The Origin

Interland Series Book #4

Gary Clark

For Grandad Peter

Author's Note:

Jay and her friends refer to the South African setting for this book as *Kaapstown*. This is a made-up combination of the English for Cape Town, and the Afrikaans word for the city, Kaapstad. There are elements of this setting in the book which the author has drawn from his knowledge of Cape Town, but there are many other elements that are pure fiction – such as the presence of the rivers flowing through the city, for example. The author hopes his combining of details from knowledge and from imagination does not jar too much with those who know Cape Town better than him, and doesn't detract from your enjoyment of the adventure.

First published 2022 GCL Books.

www.garyclarkauthor.co.uk

Paperback ISBN 978-1-8384-0105-4

The channel for Dark energy on Island 8, home of Jay, Cassie and Stitch, has been destroyed. The source stone's power on this island remains strong.

But the Dark has descended on Island 7.

The Given's young leaders must travel to Island 7 and confront the Readers before they gain permanent control.

Before they extinguish the Given power...

Chapter 1

The shock of cold sent a bolt of panic through Jay's body. She opened her arms to slow her descent. Her lungs ached. She fought to stop herself from gasping for air as she pushed herself towards the sky above the pool.

She crashed through the surface, gasping for air, treading water. The familiar tingle of power spread over her skin. She closed her eyes and relaxed. In the water of an Interland pool, the interface between her body and her surroundings was indistinct – there was little between herself and the energy of the environment.

It was the power of the Interland that allowed Jay to move between lands, from the source in her homeland, where the three rivers converged, and the source in any of the other seven lands, the *Islands*.

The landscape here was unfamiliar to Jay, a vast lake and rocky shore, but she knew from the warmth in the air that they were back in Kaapstown. The last time she'd visited Island 7, she and Toyah had arrived through the source to find themselves in the basement of a demolished building. There was a silence now deeper than mere quiet. Was this really Kaapstown — the home of Tiago, and a land under control of the Dark? Where was the City? The people?

She looked around for the others. Her saturated clothes slowed her movements. Cassie broke the surface first, pushing up into the air with the elegance of a dolphin. A few seconds later, Stitch splashed into the open, coughing and spluttering.

Cassie swam towards a protruding rock island while Jay treaded water, waiting for Stitch to catch up with her. As soon as he reached Jay's side, Stitch grabbed a hold of Jay by the shoulders, and she went under. Rising a moment later, coughing out water, Jay wriggled free of her friend's grasp. 'Get off! You'll pull us both under.'

Stitch thrashed in the water; he was an unsteady swimmer at the best of times.

'Follow Cassie,' Jay said, nodding toward the rocks. Stitch pushed off, using Jay as leverage and sending her back under. She surfaced again, spitting water, vowing silently not to wait for him next time.

The sun warmed Jay's head and shoulders. It could get hot in Kaapstown. The last time she'd been here, Readers had almost seized her and her friend, Toyah. It was one of the nearest of her near-death experiences when battling Readers.

Jay clambered out of the water, her sodden clothes dripping. She could feel the energy of the Island 7 source stone, the stone that would lie at the epicentre of Given power, charged with the energy of the confluence of rivers over millennia. The power rippled the air. Despite the energy of the stone, and despite her advanced marking of '8C', she wouldn't be able to pinpoint its location here on Island 7. To find it, she would first need to find Tiago.

Stitch lay back on a slate-grey rock, his straggly hair splayed out behind his head. He closed his eyes as he caught his breath.

'Maybe we should think about swim lessons one day?' Jay asked, looking up to where Cassie was climbing to the peak to get a better view.

'Haha funny,' said Stitch, opening his eyes and lifting himself up onto his elbows. He squinted in the sunlight. 'I'm a superb swimmer. Where are we?'

'Kaapstown,' said Jay.

Stitch frowned. Jay understood his confusion. Little made sense about the landscape. The lake stretched out into an imperfect circle of what must be a mile in diameter. There were no buildings within their line of sight — just water, and a baked orange shoreline that rose steeply to a lip some two hundred metres up.

'Where are all the buildings that were here? There were hundreds,' said Stitch.

'Flattened, I guess. Or sunk,' said Jay.

'Readers? Atta?' said Stitch.

Jay didn't answer, though she was sure Stitch was right. The Readers were the purveyors of darkness, who had come so close to destroying their own homeland, Island 8. Atta was their leader.

'Do you feel anything?' asked Jay. 'From the source stone?'

Stitch nodded. 'I feel the power, for sure. But it's indistinct. What about you? Can you feel it?'

Before Jay could answer, a call came from Cassie. 'Here,' she shouted, beckoning them to join her.

Up at the peak, Jay could see beyond the ridge to the far-away city. The City had been pushed away from the source, and the lake had sunk deeper into the earth. 'It could have been a natural process,' said Jay. 'Remember the Legend?' The Legend of Jay's dad's stories told of a crater lake at the confluence of three rivers sinking deep into the earth.

'Either that,' Cassie said, 'or the Readers have tried to destroy this Interland in the same way they did ours.'

'Whichever it is,' said Jay, 'they didn't destroy everything. The power is still here.'

'They haven't learned much, have they?' said Stitch. 'It doesn't matter what they blow up. They can't stop rivers from flowing.'

'What about the source stone?' said Cassie. 'We'll need it to stand a chance.'

Jay shrugged. 'I can feel it, but to find it, we need Tiago.'

Cassie had her hair tied back in braids. The sun glinted off her drying skin, and she stood in her familiar defiant stance — ready for action. She was a Runner, her figure seven as black as oil and displayed with pride on the inside of her wrist.

Jay smiled at Cassie's show of strength, but her happiness was short-lived. A wisp of darkness flowed through her body. It was momentary, but it was enough to remind Jay that Darkness lived on in her. If she were to win and save this land, she'd have to keep it suppressed.

Ever since the events on Island 8 just a few weeks before, when they destroyed the source of the Dark power, Jay had shouldered the burden of confusion that came with an inner combination of Given and Dark energy. She reached down and ran her fingers over the smooth skin on the inside of her wrist. Taking a deep breath, she straightened, her gaze drifting across the water. She was an 8C. She was uniquely powerful. She rejected the Dark and would not allow it space to affect her.

'Look at her,' said Stitch in a mocking tone as he regarded Cassie. 'She thinks this is going to be a walk in the park.'

Jay enjoyed Cassie's optimism, but reality nagged. This would not be easy. Something was wrong on Island 7. For one, it was eerily quiet.

On the cliff face, a gorge sliced through and a waterfall emerged from the rocks. 'That's the third river — the unnamed river,' said Stitch.

A familiar shimmer of energy rose from the spot where the waterfall joined with the lake. 'Beautiful,' said Jay. 'That's our route home, when it's time.'

'You think the source stone is under there some-where?' asked Cassie.

'Yes. But now we need to find Tiago.'

'If he's alive,' said Cassie.

Tiago, the 8C of Island 7, had been an ally to Jay and her friends, and now his land was under the threat of total control by the Dark. Tiago was alive, Jay sensed it, but if they were to help him, then first he would need to help them locate the source stone.

'I'm not sure,' said Stitch.

'About what?' asked Cassie.

'I can't see a way this plays out that ends well.' Stitch looked at Jay. His expression challenged her. 'I know we talked at length about the potential weakness of Given energy here. But. If we're going to win, Jay, you're going to have to think about using your Dark energy.'

Jay shook her head. 'It's not the way,' she said. 'It makes no sense. It pollutes my energy.'

'At least be open to the potential?'

Jay stayed firm. 'I will be more powerful without the dilution by Dark energy. It's too dangerous to dabble with it now.'

Stitch stayed silent

'I'm with Jay,' said Cassie. 'We do this with the power of the Given. It's safer.'

Jay put a hand on Stitch's shoulder and felt his anxiety as pure as if it were her own. She sent feelings of solidarity, reassurance, and support through to him. His negative energy reduced a little. 'To find Tiago, then?' she said.

Stitch nodded and stood. 'That way.' He pointed towards the near shore, to the south. Before any of them could say another word, Cassie dived into the water and, with strong, even strokes, swam towards shore. Stitch rolled his eyes at Cassie and edged towards the water, looking for a place to ease himself in.

Jay steadied herself on a ledge, checking for rocks beneath the surface, then followed Cassie. She turned to see Stitch lower himself carefully into the water and, with a combination of breast stroke and doggie paddle, make his way after her.

Chapter 2

Jay was hit first by the unexpected silence. There were no car engines, horns, squeals of brakes, or beeps of pedestrian crossings. There was no sound of humans at all. In the shelter of the buildings, even the wind was muted.

Stitch caught Jay's eye, and she read his unease. They set out along the road, three lanes of empty blacktop. White lines of futile crossing points sectioned the highway every few hundred metres into the distance. City buildings stood tall and silent on both sides of the road, like sleeping sentries.

Jay's sense of anxiety dampened a little by a feeling of awe at the sight of the deserted streets. It was like they'd been transported onto the empty set of an apocalyptic movie. Never had she experienced a city street so peaceful. No smell of smog or exhaust, the footpaths wide and uncluttered.

And then finally, the sound of a motorbike in the distance, its exhaust silencer long since blown. 'Let's get out of sight,' said Stitch. 'We know nothing about what's happened here.'

Jay and Stitch dashed for cover. The sound of the motorbike drew closer.

'Cassie!' shouted Jay. Cassie stood fixed to the spot in the middle of the road. Jolted from her thoughts, Cassie looked toward the approaching motorbike, then ran to join her friends before the noise rounded the corner.

What sounded like a powerful motorbike turned out to be a moped with no exhaust pipe. Jay almost laughed at the incongruous sight of it approaching at a snail's pace.

The moped pulled up outside a shop on the opposite side of the street. The rider was a boy not much older than sixteen or seventeen, no crash helmet, and nothing but shorts, t-shirt and sandals. He jumped off the bike and opened up the pannier box on the back, looking around to check that he was alone. He left the box open and entered the pharmacy, deserted but with its doors unlocked.

In less than a minute, the boy returned with a bag full of supplies, which he squeezed into the box on his bike and locked shut. He looked around again before jumping back onto the bike and kicking it into life. The noise of the exhaust grew as he pulled away, heading back in the direction from which he'd come.

'What's going on here?' said Stitch, stepping from cover onto the sidewalk to watch after the bike.

'Let's go,' said Jay. She'd found her way to Tiago's place before, and although she was starting from a different location in the City, somewhere she didn't recognise, she had a sense of him. Cassie and Stitch followed.

Twenty minutes walking and they'd seen no other living thing but for the occasional rat scuttling amongst the rubbish. Cassie kept a few paces ahead of Jay and Stitch, turning now and again for guidance from Jay when they came to junctions. 'How much further?' asked Stitch, already dragging his feet.

'Not far,' said Jay, also feeling the strain of walking in steaming clothes under a baking sun.

Wind occasionally whistled between buildings, and birds tittered, giving at least a semblance of hope that there might be life on Island 7 yet. The buildings were a mixture of high rises with glass sparkling reflections of the desert sun and the occasional older, more squat edifices, reminiscent of the city's older quarters. A curtain moved in one of the windows on its fifth floor. Jay kept her head down but surreptitiously eyed the window. 'Left side of the street, brown building, fifth floor window. Someone is watching us.'

Stitch immediately looked up.

'Try being subtle,' Jay snapped.

Stitch took another look. As he did so, the curtain twitched again and a face appeared. A small boy watched as they passed. Cassie strode ahead, oblivious. Stitch straightened. 'Keep going,' he said.

'There are still people here,' said Jay, relieved that whatever the Readers had done in the City, at least some people had survived. She looked again, and this time the child remained in the window. Jay raised a hand in a half wave. The little boy did the same before appearing to be pulled back into the room. The curtain dropped to cover the window.

'What are you doing?' said Stitch.

'It was just a kid. A little boy.'

'Let's just get somewhere safe,' Stitch said, speeding up and dropping into step with Cassie.

A few more minutes passed and Jay caught sight of three more wary people watching from high windows. Yet down on the streets, the silence remained absolute. Jay wondered exactly what the people were afraid of.

A sudden sense of the darkness passed through Jay like a gust of wind. She stopped dead, bending as if winded. It took a few seconds for her to catch her breath. She straightened, grit her teeth and pushed the darkness away.

Stitch and Cassie had stopped. They stood next to a steel shutter closed up to protect a shop front. As Jay reached them, Cassie held up a finger. 'Listen.' Cassie said. A scrabbling sound came from inside the shop, like someone trying to crawl along the floor.

Quiet again.

Then more scratching from a different place inside the shop. The noises were becoming louder and more urgent.

'I think we should get out of here,' said Stitch.

'Someone might be hurt,' said Jay. She opened to her power to see if she could sense anyone's thoughts or distress.

'Something doesn't feel right,' said Stitch. Before anyone could react, Cassie reached down and pulled up the steel shutter in one swift move.

A wave of rot poured over them as the floor of the shop swarmed.

Rats.

Everywhere.

They scattered away from the light. A thousand writhing bodies. Jay covered her face with her arm to keep the smell out. Cassie stepped forward, unperturbed by the smell or the sight of rats squeezing through holes and under boxes to get out of sight.

On the floor of the shop lay the remnants of dried meats, torn open packets of sugar, cereals and rotting fruit.

'Let's go,' said Stitch. Jay followed Stitch, and eventually Cassie joined them as they turned the corner.

At last, Jay recognised where they were. 'This is the street,' she said.

Chapter 3

The relentless Kaapstown heat created shimmer mirages on the street where Tiago's house stood. The townhouse windows were opaque with thick dust. The house next door was demolished, as if it had been bombed. Roof beams twisted through the tiles, most of which lay broken and scattered on the road. The Reader attacks would have focused on the most powerful of the Given. It seemed a bomb had just missed its target.

Jay closed her eyes to open to the power. Twinges of energy fizzed over her skin then faded. As they moved further away from the source, the power became weaker. With an environment blighted by the Dark, there was drought and extreme heat. Little grew and most wildlife had long perished. There was little natural power remaining to transmit energy any distance from the Interland. Back home, there was energy in everything: the trees, their network of roots through the land mass, the sea, the rivers. Then there were the hill forts, positioned around Jay's home town like a charging system, keeping the energy levels high. Here, on Island 7, Kaapstown, she struggled to find almost any energy from an environment suppressed by Reader power and natural destruction.

Jay felt no presence inside the house. 'This doesn't bode well for Tiago,' she whispered.

'Shall we knock?' said Cassie.

'We don't have to. There's no-one in there,' said Jay. She stepped to the door and gave it a shove. It didn't budge. She looked along the rows of houses on both sides of the street for signs of life, but there was nothing anywhere on the street. No twitching curtains. Yet, they still felt watched. 'We're out in the open here. Let's head around the back.'

They found an alleyway just fifty yards from Tiago's house, which led them to a pathway that ran along the backs of the houses. The walking surface was a dry, hardened mud, with little shade from the sun. As soon as they were level with Tiago's back garden, Jay recognised it.

The back of the house was like any other in the street, but the little garden, only ten feet across, was distinctive: carefully designed, loved, and tended.

Everything was in place, but for the yellow plastic trike she'd seen on her last visit, upturned at the edge of the garden, like it had been kicked aside. She pushed open the back gate, wincing as it scraped loudly over the concrete pathway.

Jay stopped and righted the little trike, brushing the dust from its seat. Stitch cupped his hands against the back window of the house and peered through. Jay joined him. Across the floor of the back room they could see a broken lamp, CD cases, papers, picture frames, a television smashed on the floor. She feared for Tiago, his wife Thabisa, and for their children, Enzo and Faith. Not only that, but if something had happened to Tiago, they would have little hope of finding the source stone. This was looking like a wasted mission.

Cassie leaned her shoulder against the back door and turned the handle. It opened with little resistance and she looked at Jay for confirmation that they enter.

Jay nodded, then stepped into the house ahead of Cassie and Stitch, anger rising inside her as she saw at close hand what the Readers had done to Tiago's home. The air was dry and musty, a layer of fine dust suspended in the filtered sunbeams. Cassie kicked at the debris that littered the floor — shards of glass, scattered books and papers, the leg of a collapsed side table.

'Stitch picked his way across the room and through to the kitchen-diner. 'It's not like they were looking for something, it's like they just wanted to smash the place up.'

'Must be Readers,' Cassie said.

Jay drew a deep breath, and with the air came feelings, images, and sounds of the darkness of Readers. In her mind's eye she saw them, merciless, and with a singular focus — to take Tiago, dead or alive, no matter what or who got in the way.

'You think they found him?' said Cassie.

A voice came from the back door, 'No.'

Jay, Stitch, and Cassie spun around, ready for action, only to see Tiago standing in the doorway, silhouetted by the bright afternoon sunshine.

It took a moment for his features to come into focus in the shadows. He was thin, his face drained of the enthusiasm Jay remembered.

'Thank God you're alive.' Jay's relief was tempered by the sense of loss she felt emanating from him. The loss he felt from the advancement of the Dark through his land was like a pulse of pain Jay could feel in her body. He surprised her by opening his arms, and she didn't hesitate a moment before embracing him.

'It's good to see you,' he said. 'We heard about what happened in your homeland.'

'Nothing compared to what's happened here, by the looks of it?'

Tiago gave a silent nod, then looked up to greet Cassie and Stitch. 'I sense these two are your closest in arms,' he said. He stepped towards Stitch. 'You are Jay's connection?'

Stitch nodded. 'We met before. In the interdimensional space. From a distance.'

'I remember,' Tiago said.

'I've been wanting to thank you for helping us,' said Stitch. 'More than once in our battles against the Dark, you gave us the power we needed to survive.'

Stitch's words took Jay back to their escape from Stitch's family home, with Readers in every room in the house. It was Tiago who created the distraction — the white light of the power of the Given — that paved the way for their escape with Stitch's dad, Samir.

'It was my pleasure.'

'I'm just sorry we couldn't do the same for you.' Stitch cast his eyes around the room at the devastation.

'Difficult to fight battles on multiple fronts, my friend.' He turned to Cassie. 'And you must be Cassie?'

Cassie gave Tiago a guarded smile and held out her hand, which Tiago shook.

Turning back to Jay, and motioning towards the front of the house, Tiago said, 'We can talk in here for a minute, then we need to move to somewhere safe.' His words confirmed to Jay that the City was not safe for the Given, and her senses became immediately heightened. Her scanning for trouble was almost subconscious. Tiago led the way into the kitchen and brushed the dust from the surface of the table before motioning for them to sit. 'I suppose it's obvious I don't live here anymore,' he said, a sad shadow crossing his face.

Tiago took a seat opposite Jay. In the light from the front windows, refracted and mottled through the dust, she could see he had cuts and bruises on virtually all of his visible skin. An older cut, now healed but sure to leave a scar, stretched down his left cheek. It reminded Jay of the type of scar that comes with a reduction — a neutralisation of a Given's power by a powerful Reader. Tiago noticed Jay studying him. He put his fingers to his cheek. 'It's been quite a battle,' he said. 'One that I'm sorry to say we have all but lost.'

'Fill us in,' said Jay. 'When we saw you, the City was functioning, the Readers were otherwise occupied, content to remain at a distance in the hills. Why did they take the City?'

'They came for me.' Tiago lowered his head, and

Jay felt the weight of his responsibility, and the sense of personal blame he shouldered for the losses in his homeland. 'And they are not interested in simply surviving alongside us; their intention is to dominate, to wipe us out.' He paused. Jay knew the Readers had no interest in co-existence. 'Atta,' Tiago continued, his tone darkening. 'I don't know what he is, but I know he has no humanity, no regard for our existence. We are nothing but an annoyance to him, something to be brushed aside.'

The thought of Atta made Jay shiver. The pain he caused was almost too much to bear, both physically as he attacked her, and emotionally as he took the life of Alf, her friend and mentor. But he had failed to take Jay's homeland. 'He's not invincible,' she said.

Tiago met her gaze. 'Something is different in you,' he said.

He was referring to the darkness inside her, a darkness he could sense. She couldn't hide it from another 8C. 'Something happened when I entered the core with Atta. There is a residual darkness that I need to purge. I am working on it. It is weak, and it is only a matter of time before my Given power is pure again.'

Tiago looked into Jay, searching. His expression was one of concern, mixed with curiosity. 'You have no reason to fear the unknown,' he said.

'I have no intention of letting this darkness remain

in me,' she said, unable to hide the sharp tone in her voice. 'I just need time.'

Stitch and Cassie exchanged a glance.

'Let's move on,' Jay said. 'If we're going to help, I need to know exactly what happened, and what we are dealing with.'

Tiago took Jay's hand across the table. 'And you?' he said. 'Will you open your mind to let me see what happened on your Island?'

Jay hesitated a moment, not confident that she could simply open her mind to others with power. She had read people many times, and she had received information through touch, but she had only imparted information a few times in this way. 'I'll try,' she said, closing her hand around Tiago's.

A stream of information hit Jay like a battering ram: pictures, sounds, smells and feelings, all smashing through at once. She gathered herself and opened her mind to Tiago, offering him the events of the past weeks in her own stream of pictures. In just a few seconds, they broke apart and Jay rocked back in her seat. The weight of the new information pushed down on her, and she kept her eyes closed for a moment.

'OK?' Tiago asked.

Jay opened her eyes and straightened in her seat. She was filled with a deep sorrow.

'I'm so sorry,' Jay said, and Tiago bowed his head.

Faith was just three years old. She had died at the hands of Readers as they hunted Tiago and his family. His pain of loss was like a tangible weight he had just passed to Jay.

He looked away, to the window, but Jay knew he saw nothing but a vision of his lost child in the reflection of his own silhouette in the dust-covered glass.

'Her death will not be for nothing,' he said with steely resolve.

They remained quiet for a moment and Jay continued to process what she had just learned. The attack of the Dark on the City had been short and decisive. They had known where Tiago was, and had come straight to his house. He sensed their approach and enacted his much studied plan for the escape of his family.

Tiago had been the last to leave the house, following his family through the maze of alleyways and side streets, just as they had planned and talked through so many times. But there was a second group of Readers who intercepted them as they emerged into the east of the City. They must have had intelligence on the routes away from his house, and had worked out their potential escape plan.

'There was something I missed,' Tiago said, reading Jay's thoughts. 'The plan, and the route away from the inner city, was good. It was a sound plan. But I missed something.'

'What?' asked Cassie.

'I've been over it a million times. I didn't anticipate their knowing exactly where we were in advance. They had time to prepare, and they had so many teams of Readers that they could close off every viable escape route.'

'What happened?' asked Stitch.

'They used guns! On children!' He paused, gathering himself. 'Thabisa was quick. She led us all through to the fields on the east side. I had Faith in my arms, so we could move quickly. Her head was buried in my shoulder. Bullets fizzed through the cornfields. I still hear them slicing through the crops just before the thud as one took my little girl. The bullet went right through my shoulder. If I hadn't been holding her, then she would never have been hit. She was dead before she could make a sound. I carried her. But I knew she was gone.'

He sat in silence, his face flushed and hands trembling.

Stitch put a hand on Tiago's arm.

'I couldn't set her down,' Tiago said. 'I just couldn't.'

'I'm sorry,' said Jay.

She sifted through the rest of the information that

had come through from Tiago. With Faith in his arms, they made it through to the underground sanctuary at the edge of the City, where there was already a community of Given in hiding. Tiago's clothes were soaked in his daughter's blood.

'Thabisa tried to use her powers of healing, but Given healers cannot bring people back from the dead,' Tiago said. 'Thabisa wailed. I've never heard a sound like it. I stayed with Faith's body for hours.'

'We should have gone into hiding in the underground earlier. As others did. I was reluctant to leave my home.'

'Why the determination to get to you?' asked Jay.

'He's the 8C,' said Stitch.

'I mean to take you. The images are clear. They wanted to take you. Why?'

'We don't know for sure. Only that it makes sense for them to eliminate any prospect of a resurgence of the Given, not that it is likely with so few Given left. But the chance remains, and who better to lead it than the 8C?'

'Even without your connected C, you are still a threat,' said Cassie.

There was something more, something Jay could not see. She could understand the drive to kill the Island's most powerful, but to take him, the reason was not clear. Maybe they would use images of the defeat of the 8C to influence the population – both Given and those without power – and show how they could not be defeated. They may have wanted to make an example of Tiago, to force people to turn over any Given they were harbouring.

'And you too have suffered,' Tiago said. 'I felt it when Alf was killed. He was a part of me too. He did much for the cause of the Given, in both your land and mine. I can see that you feel his loss deeply.'

'I exposed him to the Dark,' said Jay. 'It was my fault.' No matter how much her rational mind told her she shouldn't blame herself for Alf's death, for the way that Atta used her power to get to Alf, she couldn't help feeling responsible. She no longer talked about Alf to others. The narrative was always the same — that there was nothing she could have done, that it wasn't her fault, to let it go. It wasn't so easy to let it go.

'We've talked about this,' said Stitch. 'Alf's death was not–'

'Leave it,' Jay said, interrupting Stitch and maintaining eye contact with Tiago. Tiago nodded, acknowledging her pain once more, and allowing her to mourn Alf in her own way, for now.

'I miss his presence,' Tiago said.

Jay nodded, and the four of them remained silent for a minute.

'Tell me about this source stone,' Tiago said.

'From the literature, we learned that it's the focus of power of the Given. In our land, it was the stone at the point of confluence of the three rivers deep underground, the stone that had been imbued with Given power over many years. Here, we don't know. We hoped you might know what form it takes?' Tiago thought for a moment, and Jay could see that he knew something of the source stone. 'Is it here? Do you have it?' she asked.

Tiago shook his head. 'My girl, Enzo, she found a fragment of stone at the lake before the Readers came in force. Enzo has power developing, we know that, but she wears this tiny stone fragment as a pendant around her neck, and I can feel its energy. We assumed it was simply part of our environment, the Given power, with a particular strength of energy. I don't know. But now I think it could be a part of what you call the source stone.'

'Where is the rest of it?' asked Jay.

Tiago shrugged. 'At the lake, I guess.'

'Will the fragment be enough?' asked Stitch.

Jay had been thinking the same question — whether it might be possible that this fragment, if it did indeed turn out to be a fragment of the source stone, could be enough to threaten the core.

She shook her head. 'I don't know.'

'What was it like?' Tiago said. 'When you took

Atta and the source stone into the core, what did it feel like?' He leaned forward, his expression brightening.

She remembered dragging Atta with her into the core. The blinding mush of bright light. The piercing feeling of Given power forcing out the Dark. Then that fusing of darkness and light inside her, a feeling she was afraid to voice. Beautiful and complete. Terrifying.

'It was final,' Jay said. Tiago frowned and Jay continued. 'The feelings inside me were unambiguous. The power of the stone, with me, in the core, destroyed any possibility for Atta's power to exist in our homeland. It was final.'

Tiago nodded. 'That's good to hear. It brings us hope. What you did for your homeland is the first example of how we can defeat the Dark–'

'Not the first,' said Stitch. 'We think the same has happened for one of the other Islands.'

Jay was surprised Tiago knew nothing of previous events over at Island 4. He'd not mentioned anything in their previous meeting, but he had a deep sense of connection with the power of the Given, and could project his influence beyond the borders of his own homeland. She would have guessed that he'd have an intuition about the freedom of Island 4. Stitch explained to Tiago what Alf and Colson had discovered about the historical information recorded about the *Event* on one of the other islands, an event that they had deduced to be the destruction of the core in that land.

Tiago shifted in his seat, his eyes wide with excitement. 'This is good news!' he said. 'This means there is a way for us to succeed. We truly do have hope.'

'Yes, but first we have an almost impossible mission,' Stitch said, 'we must get the source stone into the core.'

'I felt something at your Interland,' said Jay. 'I felt the presence of your source stone. Enzo may have a fragment, but the rest of it must still be at the lake. It's a great mass of Given energy, and we will need you to pinpoint it. You are the only one who can decipher its signal with enough definition.'

Tiago frowned, as if searching his mind for a memory. 'Before their withdrawal from the City, the Readers occupied the land around my Interland for some weeks, scouring the pits, destroying and removing the buildings.'

'We saw the crater, and the lake,' said Cassie.

'Yes,' said Tiago. 'There's little left of the City in that area.'

'You think they were looking for the source stone?' said Cassie.

Tiago nodded. 'Perhaps. But they stopped. Their hundreds of Readers at the lake just packed up and left.'

'So they either found it, or they gave up,' said Cassie.

'I'd like to see Enzo's pendant,' Jay said.

A noise from the front room caught their attention. Cassie stood and edged towards the doorway. Stitch followed.

Another sound.

'Rats,' said Cassie.

Stitch jumped, knocking into some shelves and letting out a scream. Cassie laughed at his reaction.

Tiago stood. 'They are everywhere. They are like Readers. They expand into every space where there is no resistance.' He looked at his watch. 'We need to leave. The waves of Reader attack will come with the fading of the light. They prefer to come after dark. We are sitting ducks here.'

'Where are they now?' asked Stitch.

'In the northern hills. They keep close to their source of power.'

'The sink?' asked Jay.

'Yes,' said Tiago. 'You are one of the few to have seen it and still be breathing.'

Jay shivered at the memory.

Chapter 4

Tiago moved quickly through the alleyways and side streets, ducking through small gaps, over walls and under fences. He had clearly taken this route countless times and was not to be out-manoeuvred by Readers again. They shielded. Jay, Stitch and Cassie had to concentrate to keep up in the fading light without tripping or hitting their heads on low hanging obstructions.

Stitch stumbled, scraping past a stiff bush and falling on his knees with a yelp. Jay stopped and reached out a hand. 'Come on,' she said, her tone gentle. There was no time to rest; Tiago showed no signs of slowing, and Cassie remained close, keeping pace. Stitch took Jay's hand, and she helped him up, then pushed him on ahead of her. She followed, snapping at his heels.

They ran for nearly half an hour before Tiago led them from a secluded alleyway into a deserted side street that led down to an underbridge beneath a railway. The road ahead was in a cutting, with steep, grassy banks channelling them towards the bridge. The air was cooler, the surroundings greener, and Jay sensed they were on the edge of the City. In the twilight, the brick arch bridge framed a small piece of grey sky, spanning the road like the entrance to another world.

Tiago strode ahead, Cassie beside. They exchanged a few words Jay didn't catch. Stitch stopped in the road, resting his hands on his knees and looking up at Cassie and Tiago as he caught his breath. 'Those two are like machines,' he said, sweat covering his forehead.

Jay rested cross legged on the road. She was pleased to hang back with Stitch for a moment, and not sure if she'd be able to run much further if Tiago and Cassie took off again. Tiago looked back over his shoulder and jerked his head for Jay and Stitch to get moving. Jay wiped perspiration from her forehead and stood, staggering over to Stitch and grabbing him by the arm. 'Let's move it, soldier.'

As Tiago and Cassie reached the bridge, fifty metres ahead of Jay and Stitch, they ducked out of sight. Jay and Stitch exchanged a glance, then saw the small opening in the side of the bridge abutment. It was invisible from a distance, and even close up simply looked like a partly demolished section of bridge. Bricks lay in piles, concealing a route through to a lower level you'd never stumble upon by accident.

Tiago ushered them into a narrow tunnel, where russet brown soil was supported with timber props and bracing. The enclosed space was lit only by a string of orange lights stretching into the distance. Behind them, he pulled a heavy wooden panel across the entrance, securing it with thick timber beams. It gave Jay little comfort that it would resist any determined group of Readers. The Dark had its tentacles of power into all elements of Island 7, and the chances of the Given finding somewhere out of reach of their senses were low.

Tiago read Jay's concern. 'This goes deep.' He nodded down the slope of the tunnel. 'And the soil here is our friend. The subsurface vegetation stretches like a matrix through the ground. It acts as a shield to their power.'

They walked. Tiago and Jay were side by side, with Stitch and Cassie behind. Only Tiago and Cassie had to duck slightly at each supporting cross timber.

Tiago continued as they pressed deeper into the earth. 'This was first constructed some twenty years ago. It began life as a bunker. A final option for safety when all else had failed.'

'For who? The state?'

Tiago snorted. 'No. For the Given. Most of our state leaders have already been turned to Readers.'

'Forcibly?' asked Jay.

Tiago shook his head, disappointment in his expression. 'They went willingly.'

They turned a corner and the tunnel opened out into a cavern. It reminded Jay of the Interland back home. Timber props gave way to larger steel columns. Jay looked around, marvelling at the effort and determination that must have gone into transporting the larger columns deep underground. The roof of the cavern was supported by a steel frame with thick wooden beams sitting on the steel columns, some fifty feet above their heads, with a span of what Jay guessed must be over a hundred feet. The space felt similar, but bigger than their Interland cavern on Island 8, and it gave Jay a sense of comfort and safety in its familiarity. There were multiple tunnels leading away from the central cavern, but it was clear they had reached their destination.

A large table in the centre of the room looked as if it formed the focus of whatever planning and strategy talks went on in this underground bunker.

'Where is everyone?' asked Cassie.

He nodded towards the corner of the ceiling where a camera stared back at them. 'They'll be here shortly. Once they are sure you are not holding me under duress.' He smiled at the thought of it. 'If they think I am compromised, then this all comes down, and they abandon through the escape tunnels.'

'Nice,' said Stitch, looking up into the ceiling. 'Where do the escape tunnels lead?'

'Let's hope we never need to find out,' Tiago said.

A noise alerted their attention to the entrance to one of the connecting passages. A face appeared, tentatively peering around and into the room. Jay recognised Enzo, Tiago's older daughter, and now his only surviving child. Sadness hit Jay's stomach at the loss of the girl's sister. She ran into the room. 'Baba,' she squealed, flinging herself at his legs. He reached down to pick her up and turned to watch as others filed into the room from where Enzo had emerged.

Thabisa was first, Tiago's partner. She walked tall. She had a strong and defiant posture, her expression hardened by the suffering they had been subjected to, and the losses taken. Her eyes softened as she approached Jay, filling slightly, and Jay felt her deep sadness. She felt bad for bringing some of the outside back into Thabisa's consciousness, where it was clear she had been trying to keep the pain as far away as possible. Without words, Jay expressed her sorrow and her support for Thabisa. They hugged, and Jay felt her pain to her own core.

'It is good to see your face,' Thabisa said.

'I'm so sorry,' said Jay.

Thabisa shook her head. 'We need to focus now. And you are here. It is precisely what we need.' She turned and motioned towards the others, who filed into the room behind Thabisa. They spread into the space, keeping some distance between themselves and the newcomers at first, but gradually drawing closer as it became clear that they were indeed all on the same side.

'How many others?' asked Jay, looking around the room at perhaps ten or fifteen faces.

Thabisa cast her eyes around the room. 'This is it,' she said. All here are Given. And as far as we know, all other Given are either dead or converted to the darkness as Readers.'

'No,' Jay stammered. There must have been thousands of Given. They cannot all be dead, or taken by Readers. Thabisa nodded, lowering her gaze to the floor. 'I'm sorry,' said Jay.

Enzo returned and clung to her mother, eyeing Jay with distrust.

Jay crouched so that their eyes were on the same level. 'Hey,' she said, clocking the pendant around her neck. 'Your dad tells me you have been a great help and that you are strong. That's a beautiful stone. What is it?'

She looked up at her mum with a coy smile, then let go of her mum's legs so she could show Jay her necklace, a silver chain from which a green stone hung. 'Kaaps Stone,' she said. 'It's from the Interland.'

Jay looked up at Thabisa. Tiago joined them. 'What do you think?' he said. 'Is this our source stone?'

Jay had felt the power emanating from the stone as soon as Enzo entered the room. 'It is. But it's small. We need the rest of it.'

Thabisa gave Tiago a quizzical look, and he told her he'd fill her in on the details later. Another little girl appeared at Enzo's side, around the same age. Enzo smiled at her friend and was preparing to head off when Jay called her back. 'Do you mind if me and your dad have a look at your lovely stone, just for a minute or two?'

She looked at her mum, who nodded. Then she unhooked her necklace at the back, handed it to Jay, and ran off to play with her friend. As soon as the stone touched the skin of Jay's hand, she felt its power like an electric jolt. It comforted her.

Thabisa and Tiago led Jay to the edge of the room, where they took a seat. Images flowed into Jay's mind from the power of the stone. She tried to control them. She wanted Tiago to see what she saw.

'What is it?' asked Tiago.

'Take my hand,' said Jay.

Tiago and Thabisa closed their hands around Jay's, and she let her resistance go. The images flowed. At first, they were familiar: pictures of the rushing waters, stretching branches and twisting roots of the elements of the environment. Whispers came in and out of range, as if floating on the wind. They grew louder. Then the images grew darker, as if Jay was floating beneath deep water. The images slowed, came into focus. They all saw the stone. They were looking at Island seven's source stone. It appeared intact, similar to their stone on Island 8, and green in colour, just like Enzo's pendant stone. The stone lay on the bed of a river, or lake, under the water.

The images faded, and new pictures emerged. Readers. A familiar thumping sound filled Jay's ears – the sound of the rotating facility that formed the Readers' sink room on Island 7. Waves of darkness flowed over Jay. Images of Readers, hundreds of them, guarding the sink location and spreading through the surrounding hills. More Readers up in the mountains scouring the ground, walking in long straight lines casting torch light in even arcs across the garden. Mist came down over the mountaintops, cloaking the lines of Readers in a grey, murky soup.

The power of the stone was palpable. It warmed Jay's palm.

Tiago and Thabisa released Jay's hand simultaneously, and both shrunk into themselves for a moment before re-emerging like a shrivelled plant to rehydrate. Thabisa locked eyes with Jay. 'What did we just see?'

'The source stone,' said Tiago, staring at the stone pendant in Jay's hand. 'The thing that little stone came from, and the thing we need to find if our homeland is to survive.'

'What of the Readers?' asked Thabisa. 'I saw hundreds of them. What do they search for in the mountains?'

'I don't know,' said Jay. 'But we will find out soon enough. We need to head off as soon as possible, first to the lake to find the stone. We will need you for this.' She looked at Tiago. 'Then we go to the sink location.'

'We will send a team with you. I need to be there too,' Tiago said.

'No,' said Jay. 'Once we have the stone, we need you to be here. We will need to channel the power from your land, which will best come from here. The energy is still strong here, below the surface.'

Tiago looked disappointed. 'You will need soldiers with power.'

'You will have to channel the power of the Given

from here. Draw on the energy of the land, and channel it to us at the sink room so that we may fight the darkness. One team here, and one at the crater-lake.'

'Like your hill forts?' asked Tiago.

'Exactly,' said Jay.

THE FOLLOWING DAY, after a broken night's sleep in one of the specially made dorm rooms, Jay followed Thabisa's directions to the generator room, where her clothes, along with those of Stitch and Cassie, had been taken for drying the previous night. The generator room was the warmest and best ventilated in the whole of the underground bunker.

The room was noisy with the sound of the three generators, each a cube of around two metres across, supplying power to the underground network of tunnels and caverns. The majority of the overall power demand was drawn by the lighting and ventilation. The bunker was never intended for anything more than a short-term retreat for a few days or weeks. The Given holed up in the underground were already running low on supplies, requiring daily excursions into the City to top up.

As Jay pulled on a dry top over her bare torso, she

sensed a presence and turned to glimpse something in the far corridor.

Back in the main cavern, people gathered for breakfast. Tiago had asked Jay, Cassie, and Stitch to talk to those present, after breakfast, about their experiences in taking on the power of the Dark on Island 8. The Island 7 Given needed something to give them a little hope.

Across the room, Stitch and Cassie spoke animatedly to a woman. She had deep, black skin, her hair pulled back beneath a headscarf. With a bump to Jay's side, Enzo appeared, her pendant bobbing around her neck. 'Hi, Jay,' she said. 'Do you want some food?'

'Yes please, little one. Where shall I sit?'

'Next to me, here,' she pointed to a chair at the table where plates and bowls had been arranged for food, and the plans and documents cleared away.

'Where's your mum and dad?' Jay asked.

'Baba is here,' she said. 'Mamma is with Arthur, collecting supplies. She won't be back til just before dark.' Jay didn't know who Arthur was, but it was sensible for the Given to head out in groups of two rather than alone, much like the Runners used to back at their Interland.

Tiago arrived in the hall and sat on the other side of Enzo. Over breakfast, Jay took the opportunity to observe what was the last of the Given on Island 7. There were eighteen people around the table, including herself, Stitch and Cassie. And at least two were out collecting supplies. The balance of power was clear. There would be hundreds of Readers led by Atta, and no hope of the Given winning a standing fight. They would need a better plan.

'So few Given left,' Jay said to Tiago.

Tiago continued to eat. 'It's possible that one or two have taken shelter somewhere, but the knowledge of this place amongst the Given is good. If they can travel through the City, they are here. We lost many.'

Jay took a moment to take in the gravity of the facts — with less than twenty Given remaining, the losses must have been in the thousands.

Despite being outsiders, Jay felt a strong sense of solidarity with the Island 7 Given. When she caught the eye of others at the table, she felt their anticipation for a plan, something to give hope.

There were six kids, including Enzo. All under the age of ten, as far as Jay could tell. Most of the adults were in their thirties or forties, with just one boy who looked younger — twenties, maybe. He looked to be keeping himself to himself at the end of the table, his head down. Occasionally, someone spoke to him and he responded with just a smile or a nod. Jay sensed something about this boy that was unique. She could read and feel it from across the room. He caught Jay staring, and she averted her eyes. She felt her cheeks flush a little and kicked herself for being coy.

With breakfast drawing to an end, Tiago stood to attract the room's attention. People continued to murmur so Enzo stood and clapped her hands. The talking stopped and Enzo grinned at Jay, pleased by her show of power.

'Thank you, Enzo,' he said, giving his daughter a smile. 'Last night we welcomed three new guests from our sister land, Island 8. We are privileged to receive their "8C", Jay, and her connected "C", Stitch. And not least, Cassie, a level 7 Runner.' He cast his hand around to welcome the three friends.

'We have already talked through Jay's proposals, her plan for helping us to free this land as she did in her own homeland. We are under no illusions here that we are a depleted force. The number of Readers far outweighs that of the Given. But there is hope. I have asked Jay to take a little time to describe what happened on Island 8 – how they defeated the Dark and expelled Atta's influence for good. This will serve as an example to us. And, with their help, we can put a plan into place.'

Jay stood. She explained the theory of the source stone, and its ability to sever the connection between the core – the source of Dark power – and the surface, where the Readers deploy their sink technology to harness and amplify their power. She beckoned Enzo to her, and took her pendant in her hand, feeling its energy. 'This is a fragment of the source stone. Touch it. You can feel its energy. But this is not enough. We need the full stone to make the required impact on the connection.'

Murmurs spread through the room. 'How do we locate the stone?' came a voice from one of the women.

Tiago stood to join Jay. 'This is Sanata,' he said to Jay. 'She is one of just two remaining at level 7.' Sanata nodded a greeting to Jay.

'We know where it is,' Jay said.

'The stone,' Tiago said, 'is at the crater lake, where the three rivers meet. Jay and I will find it. Then it can be taken to the where the Readers draw their power.'

'The mission to the sink facility is one for me only, with my friends here,' said Jay. She smiled at Cassie and Stitch. 'You are the last of the Island 7 Given. You must remain here until we have destroyed the connection. We will need your support in channelling the power from here.'

Sanata stood again. 'I agree. If we leave the protection of the underground,' she said, 'we will not stand a chance, and the Given will be wiped from this land.' She turned to Jay. 'And what happens if you fail?'

'We will not fail.'

'They will surely destroy the source stone if they

capture you, and then what hope will be left?' Sanata asked.

'This plan is not without risk, but we have no choice.'

A young man across the room who Jay had been observing slowly got to his feet. 'The source stone cannot be destroyed by the Readers,' he said, with confidence.

'What do you know about the source stone?' Sanata snapped dismissively.

Tiago raised a hand to calm the room. 'This is Femi,' he said. 'Thabisa's cousin. He is a powerful member of the Given, and has provided great insights to the movements and incursions of the Dark. He is the son of my connection, my C, rest her soul.'

'How do you know the Readers can't destroy the stone?' asked Jay.

Femi stood, circling the table to approach Jay. 'Because it's not that simple.'

'If it can fragment,' Jay nodded towards Enzo's pendant, 'then it can surely be destroyed?'

Femi stepped closer to Jay. 'This is something that I just know.'

A wave of darkness washed over Jay and she stumbled back from Femi. 'You have darkness,' Jay breathed.

Stitch and Cassie stood, taking a protective stance. Femi put up his hands.

'What does she mean?' Tiago said to Femi. 'You are Given. I know it.'

'I am Given,' Femi said. 'But it's true I have some insight into the darkness.'

Murmurs through the room grew in volume and Femi stepped back from the group, his head lowered. Sanata spoke first. 'He could betray our location to the Readers.'

'No,' Tiago said, defending Thabisa's cousin.

'I am not a Reader. I simply have a connection to the darkness. No different to her.' He pointed at Jay. 'Tell them. You, too, have a connection. It's not a weakness, it's a strength. We can use the darkness to our advantage.'

Jay shook her head and resorted to her well-worn line. 'The darkness in me is nothing I can't expel.' She turned to face the rest of the group. 'When we purged the Dark from our homeland, the darkness fused with me during the process, but that is being corrected.' She clamped her teeth together, her jaw muscles clenched tight.

'I will help you,' Femi said to Jay, his eyes pleading. 'Take me with you, and I will help you use the full potential of the combined power of dark and light. I have been practicing...'

'No,' Jay said, her tone firm and unambiguous. 'The Dark has no place on our mission.' She felt Stitch looking at her, but avoided his gaze. She knew he would be interested in what Femi had to say. He had said to Jay before that the use of darkness by the Given does not make them a Reader, it makes them a stronger member of the Given. But this was not the time for debate.

'Look!' Femi said, pulling back his sleeve. 'I am a level 7, a Runner, like Cassie.' He looked at Cassie. 'We can work together, do what we need to do. You will need the power.'

Jay couldn't be sure she could trust him. The unique energy signal she had sensed earlier was clearer to her now. He had a level of darkness within him which Jay could not allow to influence her own thinking or distract her attention. She had trusted the darkness before, and regretted it. Lives had been endangered when Atta sent a Reader to trick Jay. She would not be led astray by the darkness again. She looked at Cassie and Stitch for their agreement. Cassie nodded. 'We can't afford to risk it,' she said.

'But,' said Stitch. 'The connection of the power... I don't know. It's more nuanced than a simple dark versus light. There's a deeper potential in managing the dark power, like at the Island 8 sink room. We can manipulate...'

'Yes!' said Femi. 'That's what I mean.'

'No,' Jay said again, then turned to Tiago. 'This is not open for more debate.'

'But—' Femi protested once more.

Tiago cut him off with a raised hand. 'Enough. This discussion is ended now.'

Just then, there was a shout from the passageway and a man staggered into the room. He was hurt, and limping badly. 'Arthur,' said Tiago, panic in his voice. 'Where is Thabisa?'

Arthur had returned from the supplies-run alone.

Chapter 5

Arthur was bleeding from cuts on his face and hands like he'd faced a spray of shards of glass. He had fallen to the floor and now lay prone, barely conscious, his eyes closed and his chest heaving.

Tiago crouched. 'Arthur. Answer me. Where is Thabisa?'

Arthur mumbled something incoherent. Someone brought him water and lifted his head so that he could drink a little.

'Please, Arthur, try to tell me where is my wife?'

'The house... she's at your house. They came from nowhere.'

'Why were you at the house? Is she hurt?'

Arthur shook his head, then winced with the pain. 'I don't think she's hurt. She wanted to pick something up from the house. She fled upstairs when the explosion ripped through the front room. It knocked me to the floor, but I escaped through the back.'

'How many Readers?' asked Jay.

'Five or six is all I saw. They were heavily armed.'

'Were you followed?' asked Tiago.

Arthur shook his head. 'No. Never.'

Tiago stood. 'I go, now.' He moved to head straight for the exit.

'Wait,' said Cassie. 'We'll come.' She looked at Stitch and he nodded.

Sanata spoke, 'I'll come too. With five of us, we stand a better chance in a fight.'

Jay agreed, but she was concerned. 'This is likely to be a trap,' she said. 'Tiago, you said they've been hunting you. This is how they try to get you.'

'I have no choice,' Tiago said, his voice firm.

'Can you try to reach her with your mind?' asked Jay, although she was doubtful of his chances in the reduced power of Island 7. The source itself was strong, but the surrounding land above ground was depleted, almost like a drought had settled in, and the energy in the earth had been pushed deep underground.

He shook his head. 'I can feel her. She is alive and hurt.'

'Then we need to go. Quickly,' said Jay. 'Do you have any weapons here?'

Tiago shook his head. 'We have the element of surprise at least, and we will connect our power. I just pray that Thabisa is still there.'

~

THE AIR on the outside was cool, the sun cloaked behind thick clouds. As they approached the house, the silence was foreboding. It was too quiet. Jay sensed the power of the Dark. There were Readers lying in wait for them, she just couldn't tell how many.

They crouched in the undergrowth a few hundred feet north of the house. Jay insisted they take a moment. 'We have to try to sense them,' she said. 'I feel little darkness, but they are probably shielding.'

'I feel nothing,' Cassie said.

'Me neither,' said Sanata. 'They might have moved on. I can feel Thabisa. She is here, or was here.'

They were quiet for a moment. Jay put a hand on Stitch's arm and they made eye contact. He understood her intention and allowed his power to flow through her. Their ability to connect had strengthened over the past few weeks, and the combining of the 8C and the C was now seamless, immediate. Jay closed her eyes and pushed her vision into the ground, through to the remaining wisps of Given energy that resided below them. The power was intermittent. For too long, the Reader energy had dominated the flow of power on Island 7, and it was difficult to achieve a clear vision.

Jay made a grunting sound, breaking her grasp on Stitch. 'It's no good,' she said. It was like trying to push a boat out in a dry river.

'We know enough,' said Tiago, edging forward through to the pathway that led around to the back of his house.

'Wait,' said Jay. 'Let's go in two groups. You and Sanata around the back, we three will take the front entrance.'

Tiago nodded.

Stitch said, 'They'll be watching.'

Jay shrugged. 'We are driving blind. If they are watching the house, then they will see us whichever way we enter. Our only chance is to move quickly, get Thabisa, and defend with as much power as we can collectively muster.'

'I don't like it,' said Stitch.

'We have no choice,' said Tiago, his voice edgy.

Cassie stood. 'Let's do it.'

They approached in two groups as Jay suggested, keeping their heads below the height of the fences that bordered the pathways. Jay and her group peeled away from Tiago and Sanata, and made their way through to the road, where they would approach from the front. As they walked, the strength of dark energy seemed to falter and Jay hoped for a moment that she might have been reading it wrong; perhaps there were no Readers.

'You could try–' Stitch started.

'What?' said Jay.

Stitch kept his voice low and calm, little more than a whisper. 'We have to know what we're walking into. If the Given energy is low, the Dark power is strong. Stop being stubborn. Tap into it.'

Jay stopped and grabbed Stitch by the arms. 'I can't just switch into the Dark energy. We don't know what that will do. Don't accuse me of being stubborn. I'm being pragmatic. '

'Come on!' Cassie called in a loud whisper from ahead. 'Quit talking.'

Stitch shook his arms free. He was frustrated by Jay's refusal, but understood how dangerous it might be for her to access the Dark. They crouched at the end of the alleyway, looking out into the deserted street. Tiago's house on the ground floor had been reduced to rubble. The front wall, with door and windows, was missing, and the staircase to the first floor was visible. It wasn't clear what was holding up the top floor and the roof. Cassie pointed at the houses opposite Tiago's house, the windows dark, no sign of movement. 'If they are watching, then they're probably in there.'

They scanned the street for the safest approach. Cassie pointed out the connected front gardens of the adjoining houses. They could pass through the gardens and get close to the open front of Tiago's house without breaking cover if they kept low.

'Let's do it,' said Jay, and led the way.

They climbed over the fence into the final garden and Jay stepped down in Tiago's front yard. Now visible to any watchers, she stood and looked over to the houses opposite while Cassie and Stitch scaled the fence and joined her.

'What?' said Stitch, following her gaze across the street.

'I can't see anything. Any sign of Tiago?' she asked, not breaking her gaze over the street.

'Not yet,' said Stitch.

'Cassie,' Jay said. 'You and Stitch see if you can locate Thabisa.'

'What are you going to do?' Stitch asked.

'I need to keep watch for a minute. I'm shielding as best I can. It might give us a little more time.' Cassie and Stitch headed towards the stairs. Jay continued to tap into as much of the Given energy as she could to feed her shield and ready herself for Readers.

Cassie and Stitch disappeared up the stairs. A noise from the back of the house alerted Jay to Tiago and Sanata's arrival. She raised a hand so that Tiago could see her. 'Any resistance?' Jay asked.

Tiago shook his head, then looked towards the stairs. All three of them followed Stitch and Cassie. Jay kept a focus on the houses opposite for a further minute before turning and climbing the stairs to join the others.

No sign of Thabisa.

Tiago moved quickly to the window and crouched, scrutinising something on the floor. He brushed his fingers over the floor and brought them up to see.

Blood.

'Thabisa?' said Jay.

Tiago's anger rose, and he looked like he would explode. 'They've hurt my wife,' he said, his voice quaking with rage.

'Not enough to kill her,' said Jay. She dragged Tiago's attention from his pain and anger. 'Look,' she said. 'Whatever happened here, there is not enough blood for us to conclude that she's dead.'

Tiago turned back to the floor and closed his eyes. Jay saw his thoughts rushing through his head. Images of Thabisa popped into Jay's mind as Tiago searched for her.

'You're right,' he said. 'She's alive. I think she's at the lake.' He jumped to his feet and ran for the stairs.

'Wait,' said Sanata. 'Why would they take her there?'

'The source stone,' said Stitch. 'They're using Thabisa to draw Tiago. He's the only one who can locate the stone.'

TIAGO SET A RUNNING pace to the crater lake. It was all the others could do just to keep up. When Jay called out for him to stop so they could make a plan, he didn't even slow, just waved his hand impatiently. 'Keep up. We're running out of time.'

The group only stopped when they were crouched at the rim of the crater, looking down on the waterfall, where the unnamed river burst from the rock face and plummeted into the water below. Water spray formed clouds that filled the air, caught on the wind and cooled Jay's skin. She put a hand on Tiago's shoulder and he turned, a finger to his lips. He nodded towards the crater below. Thabisa was there, laying amongst the rocks. Even from a distance, Jay could see that she was bleeding from a serious-looking gash on her lower leg, and she held her side, blood seeping between her fingers. Her eyes were closed.

Tiago moved toward the lip of the crater, but Jay grasped his arm. 'Wait!'

He tried to shrug her off, desperate to reach his wife.

'Listen to Jay,' said Sanata. 'This is a trap. We go straight in there and none of us comes out.'

Tiago turned back to Jay. 'Be quick,' he said.

Thabisa lay in the worst possible location for them to get to. It was the perfect position for an ambush. She cast her eyes along the ridge. There were no Readers that she could see, and none that she could feel. But they would be there somewhere, she was sure of it. 'How is your power here?' asked Jay, sensing that her own power was strong, so close to the source.

'I feel good,' said Tiago.

'Me too,' said Sanata.

'We need to connect. We cannot do this as individuals. If we stand any chance of getting Thabisa out of there, we need to act as one.'

'Agreed,' said Tiago, and he held out a hand for Jay. She took his hand and motioned for the others to join.

White light flooded Jay's mind, and her head filled with whispers. The feeling of the power flowing through her was like a current. She had to focus to keep from falling over. Tiago's hand on her shoulder steadied her. Stitch's energy came through the clearest. He had fear inside him, both for his own safety and for Jay. The most powerful emotion amongst the group was that from Tiago, a trembling red hot impatience to get to Thabisa, ringed with ice cold fear for her safety.

Tiago broke the chain 'Now. It's time. We'll go down in pairs,' he said. They split into three groups. Cassie and Sanata would approach from the north, Jay and Stitch from the south, and Tiago would take the direct route.

'Keep focused,' said Jay. 'If we concentrate, we maintain the connection.' Tiago nodded, already scrambling down the rock face towards Thabisa.

Cassie and Sanata approached from the north while Jay and Stitch scanned the area, looking for signs of movement. Wisps of darkness moved around the crater, but they were too flimsy to use to pinpoint a source. Were the Readers here waiting to pounce, or had they just dumped Thabisa and moved on?

Jay and Stitch breached the edge of the crater. Tiago was already just a few feet from Thabisa. Cassie and Sanata were half way to joining him, and still there was no sign of any Readers. 'I don't like it,' said Jay.

'Keep moving,' said Stitch. 'And keep your eyes open.'

They reached Thabisa. Her eyes were closed, and Tiago had a hand on her forehead. Cassie and Sanata stood with their backs to the couple, eyeing the rocks for any approach by Readers. Tiago spoke softly to his wife. Thabisa's eyes remained closed as Tiago held her and checked her pulse. Something moved on the ridge in the mist of the spraying waterfall.

Thabisa opened her eyes. 'Tiago,' she said, her voice weak. 'You shouldn't have come. I tried to reach you with my thoughts. You shouldn't have come.'

'Let me see,' Sanata said, peeling back Thabisa's hand from her side. As she did, blood flowed and Sanata returned Thabisa's hand to press on the wound. 'Keep it there. We will tend to it back at the camp.'

'We need to move,' said Jay, not averting her eyes from the ridge.

'Can you walk?' Tiago said to Thabisa.

'Leave me,' she said. 'I'll slow you down.' She drifted away for a moment, her eyelids drooping. Then she opened them and took her husband's hands in hers, leaving them dark with her blood. 'The Readers are here.'

Jay already knew, she felt it. The Readers had come out from behind whatever shield they had constructed, and were closing in from all sides. She looked down at the lake, its still surface a mirror of the sky above, but dark. 'Are we safe?' Stitch said, his voice tight. 'Or are they here?'

'We need to leave,' Jay said, nudging Tiago. 'Now!' She leaned down and took Thabisa under the arm, motioning for Tiago to take the other arm. Thabisa moaned, but she staggered to her feet. Sanata took Jay's place on the other side of Thabisa and Jay returned her attention to the encroaching darkness, picking the direction that she felt had the weakest sense of dark power. 'That way,' she said.'

The Readers presence was like a swarm: they were shifting positions, fanning out to encircle the group. There was more movement now; every few seconds she saw something on the ridge. 'Go quickly,' Jay shouted.

An object like a piece of fruit flew towards them from the ridge. It hit the rocks just a few feet away, and the blast wave knocked Jay forward into Stitch. She and Stitch fell, sliding a few feet down the rocks, closer to the lake. Jay's ears rang with a high-pitched squeal from the explosion. She knocked her head on a rock and her vision blurred.

Her eyes open a crack, Jay saw another flash of light, then another. Explosion after explosion rang out. It was as if the Readers were determined to eliminate them without room for failure, leaving no chance of survival.

Another explosion before an ear-splitting roar as the force ripped through the rocks, throwing fragments and dust into the air.

The world went black.

Some indeterminate time later, as Jay came to consciousness, she felt no presence of Stitch or the others. Somewhere far away, she heard voices. Her eyes burned but when she tried to move her hand to her face, she found she was pinned to the ground, unable to shift her limbs. She blinked away dust and focused. A crack of light filtered through from somewhere high up above. Pain radiated from every inch of her body and her head swam. Her vision blurred. She closed her eyes and drifted away.

The next time she woke, there was silence. 'Stitch?' she said aloud, her voice a cracked whisper in her hoarse throat. She sensed him. She struggled again to keep her eyes open. Rocks moved above her head.

Voices.

'She's here.' It was Stitch. Then she heard Cassie as they scrabbled at the rocks above her head, working together to move the bigger boulders.

At last, she felt Stitch's hand in hers. 'Jay!' came Stitch's voice. His touch brought a spark of energy and her eyes snapped open as if her lungs had been freed and she could finally breathe.

'Where's Tiago?' Jay breathed.

Stitch shook his head. 'I'm sorry.'

Jay felt a deep hole open within her as she tried to take in this reality. Tiago was dead. Another loss for his family to bear. And the whole of the Island. Tiago was the backbone of Given power on Island 7. His death would not only weaken his homeland, but would also weaken the whole of the Given.

'Thabisa?' Jay asked.

'Alive,' said Stitch as he supported Jay. Cassie took her other arm and together they raised her from the hole in the ground. 'Sanata has taken her back to the underground, which is where we need to get to before any Readers return.'

Something was wrong. Jay sensed a deep sorrow and fear in Cassie and Stitch, something more than the loss of Tiago, a fear for something deeper. 'What is it?'

Stitch and Cassie exchanged a look. Jay stopped and waited. 'The source stone,' said Cassie.

'What about it?' asked Jay.

'They have it,' said Stitch. 'Tiago had no choice. It was the stone, or it was Thabisa.'

Jay's heart sank further. Not only was Tiago dead, but the only means of defending Island 7 was now in the hands of the Readers.

Chapter 6

Stitch and Cassie dragged Jay back to the underground sanctuary, where she continued to drift in and out of consciousness. Sanata had managed to get Thabisa back, although when they arrived she was in shock, mumbling incoherently about Tiago. She insisted he was alive, but Stitch knew otherwise. The Readers had carried his body away; he felt nothing of his life force.

They laid Jay down on the floor of the main cavern. People gathered, bringing water and medical supplies. Thabisa drank greedily and revived a little. Cassie flopped onto the floor, exhausted from bearing most of Jay's weight on the journey back.

Jay's breathing was shallow and her pulse weak. Stitch looked at Thabisa and she returned his gaze with a fearful expression. 'Help me,' said Stitch.

Thabisa took a breath and pushed herself up to join Stitch at Jay's side. She placed one hand on Jay's forehead, the fingers of her other hand on her neck. 'She's drifting away,' she said.

'No,' said Stitch, and placed his hands on Jay's head. 'Help me,' he said again to Thabisa. Thabisa had the powers of a healer, as did Stitch. Jay had told him that Thabisa's healing was powerful. 'I know you're weak but you have to try. Please.' Thabisa smiled weakly. She'd been bandaged and her bleeding had stopped, but she was far from full strength.

Thabisa placed her own hands on top of Stitch's and closed her eyes. Stitch immediately felt her power channel through him and combine with his own. His hands became warm.

Jay twitched beneath their touch. Thabisa began to sway and hum, her eyes rolled back in her head. Her hands squeezed Stitch's, pushing her power into Jay.

After a minute, Jay turned her head and pulled away from their grip. She gulped the air as if coming up through water to breathe again. Then she coughed, gagging slightly as she pushed herself to a sitting position. Stitch placed a hand on her shoulder. 'Easy,' he said. 'Rest.'

Jay felt as if she'd just swum up to the surface from a great depth. 'Thank you,' she said, leaning back against the wall of the cavern and inspecting herself for damage. 'Tiago?' she said, almost to herself, as if trying to remember.

Thabisa shook her head to confirm what Jay already knew. 'They took him.'

Jay looked at Stitch, who gave a slight shake of his head. He was certain. Tiago had been killed. He'd seen it with his own eyes. After the barrage of explosions, the Readers made directly for Tiago, ignoring the rest of them. Jay was buried beneath rubble. Sanata and Thabisa lay motionless. Cassie lay amongst the rubble, just a few feet from him, but unmoving. Stitch was dazed and with pain shooting through his body from the hits he took from scattering rocks.

Two of the Readers pulled Thabisa over to where Tiago lay. Thabisa was unconscious, but the Readers dug into her mind. She squirmed on the floor, Tiago screaming for them to stop. Stitch had tried to summon the strength to bring some shielding to Thabisa but got nothing. Cassie lay motionless next to him.

Stitch hadn't heard the discussion between the Readers and Tiago, but the thrust was clear. They dragged him to his feet and led him to the edge of the lake, where he closed his eyes. Stitch had felt Tiago connecting with the source, could sense him searching for the epicentre of its energy, the charged stone that had resided at the point of confluence – the source stone. In just a few seconds, he had directed the Readers to its precise location, and three of them retrieved it. Like their own source stone, this one was only a foot in diameter, and from a distance its surface looked smoothed by the decades of erosion. It sparkled in the sunlight with a green shimmer before the Readers placed it in a bag and took it away.

Stitch held his breath as one of the Readers raised his rifle and pulled the trigger. Tiago hit the floor, blood pouring from a wound to his chest. Another shot came as Tiago lay on the floor, and his movements stopped. They rolled him onto his front and lifted his body onto the back of the biggest of the Readers, then made their way back to their Land Rovers.

'He's alive,' Thabisa said. 'I feel it.'

Jay looked at Stitch but he averted his eyes. She sensed that Thabisa's certainty came from hope rather than a true feeling of Tiago's life force.

'We will find him,' Jay said, placing a hand on top of Thabisa's. Then to Stitch, 'Why do you think they took him?'

Atta wanted proof. 'If he is alive,' Stitch said, stealing a glance at Thabisa, 'then perhaps they will use him as leverage to end this, to bring the Given into submission.'

'We leave now,' said Jay, struggling to stand but falling on her knees as her legs gave way. She cried out in pain as blood seeped from a long gash below her knee.

'Recover first,' said Thabisa. 'Then we get a team together and go in force.'

Stitch reached for Jay, helping her to stand. 'Thabisa is right,' he said. 'We're no use to anyone like this.'

Jay hung her head. 'They can't destroy the source stone.'

'They'll already be back in their lair,' Stitch said. 'We stand a better chance if we can muster a strong attack.'

Cassie dragged herself off the floor to join them, then slung an arm around Stitch. 'Good work, man,' she said. 'She's heavier than she looks,' she smiled at Jay.

'It's all muscle,' Jay said, forcing a smile.

'What happened back there?' Cassie said. 'We should never have gone in like that.'

'It was Tiago,' Thabisa said. 'He did it for me. I am sorry for that.'

Cassie lowered her gaze and nodded gently.

'Let's talk later,' said Jay. 'Make a plan of action?' She turned away and staggered to leave the cavern. 'Stitch, help me out here.'

Stitch offered an arm and a shoulder for Jay to lean into. Thabisa leaned down to pick up the bag of medical supplies and handed them to Stitch. 'Take these.'

They staggered from the room together, Stitch sensing that Jay was in more pain that she let on, and fearful that the next leg of this journey now had an extra complication they hadn't banked on.

It was 24 hours before Jay was well enough to leave her bunk. Stitch and Thabisa tended to her wounds, but there was something deeper inside that needed time to heal. Ordinarily, the hill forts, or the Interland back home would speed up her healing, and her regaining of strength, but there was no such flow of Given energy in the underworld of Island 7.

Jay had swung her legs out of bed before Stitch arrived with breakfast, at last ready to stand, and determined to test her strength without an audience. She stood and stretched her arms back. Physically, she felt strong. She dressed quickly and sat back down on her bed, closing her eyes to connect with her power.

In the silence, she opened herself to the energy of the surrounding soil. It was weak, but it was detectable. The power on Island 7 was nothing like back home, and this worried her more than she allowed herself to consider. If the energy was so weak, when they came up against the Dark, and Atta, at the location of the core, then how would they even find the stone, let alone get it into the core? She pushed the doubt out of her mind and connected more deeply with the power. Whispers came in bursts, as if subdued by some unseen resistance.

Stitch ambled into the room, tray in hand. 'You're up?' he said.

Jay smiled. Her head was clear after her connection with the power, however slight, and the sight of Stitch was a welcome one. 'I'm good. And... thanks.'

'What for?'

'Looking out for me.'

'Jeez. What choice do I have, eh? Your dad and Sammy would kill me if I came back without you. That was just self-preservation.'

'Ah I see,' said Jay, laughing.

'It's good to see you laugh.' Stitch put the tray on the bed with steaming hot coffee and a delicious-looking bowl of fruit.

'Can we take that in the hall with the others?'

'If you're up to it?'

'You bet.' Jay stood and leaned to pick up the tray but Stitch grabbed it and led her out into the passageway down to the main cavern. A noise of rushing water reverberated through the stone passageways. 'What is that?' Jay asked Stitch. 'That noise has been in my head and I can't figure what it is.'

'Thabisa said there's an underground river that flows out from beneath these caverns and into the bay. It's their alternative escape route should the security be breached. There are boats down there.'

'How many?' asked Jay

'No idea, but more than are needed for the few who made it down here.' Stitch pressed on to the dining area, and Jay followed, whilst picturing the source of the noise she could now place. In recovery in her bunk, she hadn't been able to figure if the noise was real, or if it was simply the blood pumping through her veins, echoing in her ears.

Cassie and Thabisa both stood as Jay entered the cavern. Cassie spoke first. 'Sleep well?' she asked in a friendly sarcastic tone. 'Twenty-four hours isn't bad.'

'I feel hungover,' said Jay.

Thabisa led Jay to a seat and the four of them sat down. Stitch pushed the tray in front of Jay and she took a sip of coffee. Her face and shoulders relaxed as she took in the hot liquid. 'Ah, that's good. We can leave this afternoon?' she said, checking the reactions of Thabisa and Stitch.

Thabisa shook her head. 'Tomorrow. First light. We don't want to be travelling through the hills in the dark.' Enzo ran over to see Jay, sliding her arms around her waist. 'Careful,' said Thabisa. 'She is still recovering.'

'It's OK,' said Jay, draping an arm over Enzo's shoulder. In her bones, Jay sensed that Enzo already knew the truth about her father. Enzo slid away, back to her friends on the other side of the table, her expression dark. With Faith no longer here, and Tiago dead, Thabisa needed to stay safe, if only for Enzo's sake. She caught Thabisa's eye and opened her mind, allowing the grieving mother to read her thoughts.

Thabisa looked defiant at first, with thoughts only for finding her husband, dead or alive. Then she looked at Enzo, at the small child tucked in beside Jay who could so easily become an orphan, then reluctantly nodded her agreement. 'What about my cousin, Femi?'

Jay looked over to see that Femi was regarding them, as if waiting for an instruction. 'We can't endanger anyone else. We know what's needed.' When Jay looked again, Femi kept his head lowered as if he'd heard her conclusion. It brought mixed feelings in Jay. She sensed his power was significant, and he would be useful. But she didn't trust him. She couldn't understand his open acceptance of his darkness.

'I'm not sure about this,' Stitch said to Jay, keeping his voice low.

Jay sighed.

'I just mean that maybe we should take time out,

head back and see Colson and Angie. We need time to talk this through.' Since they'd lost Alf in the encounter with Atta, Colson was the greatest source of knowledge on the Given and the powers. And Angie, at just 10-years-old, was a source of immense power and the only person, apart from Stitch, who could penetrate Jay's consciousness from a distance.

'It won't make any difference,' piped Cassie, her tone confrontational. 'We can go back and talk about it, or we can get on with it.'

'If we go in unprepared, we lose,' said Stitch. 'This is Atta, remember? He'd kill us just for fun. Last time we had a well-worked plan. We had people at the hill forts. We prepared. And even then, we only just made it.'

'Exactly,' said Cassie. 'So this time we know what's needed. And, like Jay said, we can make use of the power that can be channelled from the source here on Island 7, and the power in this underground.'

'It's weak. You know it is.'

Jay put a hand on Stitch's shoulder to cool the confrontation. 'I'm worried that if we take the time needed to get back to our homeland to talk this through, we will be too late.' Jay then turned to Cassie. 'But, Cassie, Stitch is right. This is going to be a huge test. We need to think it through.'

'I know, I'm not saying–' Cassie started.

'It's OK. We are all on the same side here. Let's work it through with Thabisa and her team, then we leave in the morning like Thabisa suggests. OK?'

I will stay here,' said Thabisa. 'And we will organise a team to head to the source, to help channel whatever power we can.'

Cassie nodded.

Stitch lowered his head. He picked at his breakfast.

'Pass me the coffee,' Jay said to Stitch, trying to snap him out of his contemplation. He reached for the coffee pot, passing it to Jay. 'OK?' she said.

Stitch nodded. 'Yes, I'm in. It's just...'

'What?'

Nothing,' Stitch said, like he had checked himself. 'We can do this.'

Jay took the coffee and poured some for Stitch and some for herself. She knew they faced a near impossible battle ahead, but they had no choice but to trust they would do enough. Their first objective would be Tiago. She needed to be sure he was dead. Then they could focus on the source stone.

'We will send a communication when we figure out what's going on. Then we can fix a time for the channelling of power,' said Jay.

'You send the message. I will be open to your signals,' said Thabisa.

'Once the channel to the core is destroyed,' Jay said

to Thabisa, 'the people here can come out of hiding, and you can begin rebuilding the City.'

Thabisa tried to smile, but any positivity was tempered by her concern for Tiago. Stitch, too, looked less than convinced it would be as simple as Jay made out. He looked up at Cassie, and then to Jay, forcing a half-smile before turning back to his half-eaten breakfast.

Chapter 7

Cassie led the way through the City streets. The sun had not yet risen above the low-rise buildings in the east, and the air was refreshingly cool. Jay followed a few steps behind the group.

Stitch lagged too, and Jay could sense his annoyance. If she slowed to let him catch up, he hung back further. He used to do this when they were kids, get pissed off with her and sulk. She needed to set things straight with him. If they weren't aligned in every way, their already weakened power would be weaker still. There was no time for disagreements.

As the City sprawl thinned towards the west and north, they trudged through the suburbs of Kaapstown. The single-storey houses were smaller but in better condition than the dwellings closer to the centre. The presence of people was tangible. It was likely that the focus of Reader waves of attack would have been in the City centre. These outlying areas may have been sheltered from the worst of the Dark.

Cassie stopped in the street just ahead. Jay and Stitch caught up with her. 'What's up?' asked Jay.

'Something's wrong. It feels strange,' said Cassie.

Jay knew what she meant. The presence of more people brought a certain energy to the air, even though Jay sensed there was no power in them — neither light nor Dark. She opened more deeply for a moment, her chest swimming with the little energy signals from the environment. 'It's their fear,' Jay said. 'That's what we can feel.' She opened her eyes.

'What exactly are they afraid of?' Stitch asked.

'The Readers have drilled terror into these people. They no longer know what they're afraid of. People have no idea when they'll be taken or who is under suspicion so they live in fear. It's an effective tool of oppression.'

'Yes, I feel that,' said Cassie. 'This place is a war zone, and all these families might as well be under house arrest.' She stepped forward, resuming their journey.

'What are they going to do?' said Stitch.

'Most have already left,' said Jay. 'They've been pushed out to the borders and into neighbouring territories. I expect they are getting as far away from Kaapstown as they can, away from the influence of the Dark.'

'And these people? The ones that are still here?'

'If we achieve our goal, then they will get their lives back.'

'And if we don't?'

'Then those who can will follow the others and flee.'

'Mass migration,' said Stitch.

Jay thought about the vast numbers of Kaapstown residents who must have already migrated to other parts of South Africa, and even beyond. Either that or been killed, or transformed to Readers. Clearly, many remained, perhaps hoping for something or someone to come and face up to the Readers — a resurgence of the Given — or perhaps not strong enough to make the journey to leave their homes.

Stitch walked on, and Jay paused for a moment, feeling the flutters of energy and fear flowing through the air. She turned to look at where they'd come from. Something moved in the shadows behind them and she guessed that there were kids scurrying between gardens, curious of the visitors passing through like drifters. She vowed to herself that she'd do everything in her power to help to free these people from the influence of the Dark.

The suburbs of Kaapstown ended abruptly at a dry riverbed. One side was the City, the other comprised arid plains for a mile or two before morphing into the foothills of the mountains. Jay recognised the landscape, and in particular the hills in the distance, beyond which the Readers' lair was situated.

A natural bund of earth formed a bridge over the dry river, and linked to the pathways pressing further west and north. They would have to walk in the open between the river and the foothills. They'd be visible to anyone looking out from the hills. She looked north, following the line of the dry river basin. It was a longer route, but the dry bed was a good fifty feet below the ground surface and would easily hide them from view. They could make it all the way through to the hills without being exposed.

Cassie followed Jay's gaze and nodded her agreement. She side-stepped down the bank and onto the dry riverbed, kicking at the dust. 'This hasn't seen water for some time,' she said. Jay and Stitch followed, joining Cassie and moving off toward the hills.

The sun was high in the sky, its rays beating down on them as they dragged themselves through the thick, humid air.

They walked along the line of the river for almost an hour before they came across shade. Up ahead, a small copse of trees stood on the west bank, curving over at the top like a parasol to shade most of the width of the river basin as well as the whole of the west river bank. Jay squeezed her dry eyes half closed to focus better. It looked as if, in the basin, the river bed had water. Cassie clocked it at the same time and gave a short yelp of relief as she sped up, almost sprinting by the time she reached the water.

Cassie splashed through the shin-deep water, spraying the cool liquid up and over herself as Stitch and Jay waded in after her. Jay leaned down and cupped water into her hands to pour over her head, not sufficiently confident to drink it, but aching with relief from the heat. Cassie kicked water at Stitch and Jay, laughing. Stitch stood and allowed himself to be soaked through, a smile at last forming on his lips.

Jay took a seat under the tree on the bank and pulled her water bottle from her rucksack, along with some of the fruit Thabisa had packed for them. Cassie and Stitch continued to muck about in the water after throwing their bags onto the bank. By the time they joined Jay for a rest and a drink, they were both drenched to the skin. Stitch pulled off his soaked t-shirt and hung it over a low branch. Cassie then did the same, sitting down next to Jay in her vest top. She scraped her braided hair back into its hair band and rubbed her face with her hands. 'That felt good,' she said.

They rested, the water evaporating from their skin, cooling them in the shade of the trees. Jay leaned with her back up against one of the trees and closed her eyes. She almost dropped off to sleep, drifting away into a sea of racing thoughts and images before coming to with a start. Her eyes snapped open. Stitch and Cassie were talking together a few feet away. There was no sound but their lowered voices and the wind in the leaves above their heads. A wisp of darkness tickled at the inside of her head.

Something moved in the distance, on the bank of the river just a few hundred feet back. She knew immediately it wasn't an animal. Someone was close. She opened herself to the power of the land and directed her senses toward what she saw.

'Cassie...Stitch,' Jay whispered without taking her attention away from the direction of the intruder. Cassie loped over to Jay and looked up in the direction of Jay's gaze.

As they watched, the figure crossed over the river and into an alcove in the river bank where the earth had been scoured away. Cassie pulled herself up into a crouching position, then scampered across the riverbed to the opposite bank, avoiding the pool of water.

'Where's she going?' asked Stitch.

'There's someone there,' Jay said.

Cassie scrambled up the bank, keeping as low as

she could as she stalked back towards where the figure had disappeared into the side of the river bank.

'Shall we go with her?' asked Stitch. But it was already too late. Cassie was within metres of the intruder.

Jay and Stitch stood for a better view. Cassie half ran, half fell back down the bank and seemed to launch herself into the air. A figure in black then came into view as Cassie landed on him with force. He lay sprawled on the ground. Jay and Stitch took off along the river bed towards the scrappy fight that ensued.

'Stop!' Jay shouted as she reached Cassie and her opponent. She recognised Femi, cousin of Thabisa, the boy they had spoken with back at the underground. She felt his power. Cassie and Femi remained clamped together in combat, holding each other and ready to fight.

Cassie looked at Jay, then back at Femi as she pushed him away from her. Femi tripped backwards and landed on his backside in the dust. He stayed down, his head lowered as if ashamed to have been caught.

'What are you doing?' Jay asked him.

He slowly raised his head. 'I can help you. If you let me...'

'Not a chance,' said Cassie. 'I thought our answer was quite clear back at the cavern.'

Stitch remained quiet, looking to Jay to figure out what to do. Jay took a moment to read whatever she could from Femi. Her senses told her not to trust him. He was a self-confessed user of dark energy, something she wouldn't take lightly. He also displayed an arrogance that got under her skin.

'You have a sense of the Dark that I don't trust,' said Jay. 'For this reason, I can't accept your joining us. You need to head back to the others.'

Femi's expression turned to one of anger, but he remained quiet. Jay sensed he wanted to scream, to convince them they needed him. He mumbled a few words Jay didn't catch. Cassie snorted. 'Speak up, little boy,' she said.

Femi scowled at Cassie, then stood and brushed down his clothes, dust billowing. 'You don't get it,' he said to Jay. 'I heard what you did back on Island 8, but this is different. There is no strength in the Given energy here. You know that.' His anger bubbled below the surface and he was working hard to contain it.

'We have no choice but to try,' said Jay. 'You have a darkness in you that will be unpredictable when we are faced by Readers.'

'So do you,' said Stitch, speaking for the first time. Femi looked at him, his expression turning to one of hope.

'Stitch–' Jay started.

Stitch interrupted, 'He's one of the Given, we know that, right? And he has a deeper understanding, and possibly a connection with the darkness, a bit like you. And we know there's a potential gain to come from the combination, like you said before, the amplification of your senses after the Event. Yes?'

Jay nodded again, lowering her gaze as she contemplated once more the risk of the presence of Femi, and the threat that might come from his tendency to open to the darkness. Her thoughts became muddled with conflict. Her sense was that allowing the darkness to flow inside her was wrong, especially as they hunted for the source stone, which was a symbol of the purity and strength of Given power. But a gut feeling nagged that there was potential for strength in the combination of Dark and light. She looked at Cassie. Cassie shook her head, her opinion on the matter crystal clear.

Jay felt Stitch's worry for the likely failure of their mission. The inevitability of it seemed to ooze from him. Femi was different. He was defiant. 'You're going to come along for the ride no matter what we say, aren't you?'

Jay didn't wait for an answer. 'The first time you give any indication of being in opposition, or even just getting in the way, then you're gone. Do we have an agreement?'

Femi agreed. He looked at Stitch and gave him a

nod of thanks. Cassie snorted a derisive noise and turned on her heels to head back to the cover of the trees.

THEY WALKED for another two hours in the scorching heat of the afternoon sun before reaching the foothills and the shade of the chestnut trees. Femi had kept his distance, walking a good way behind Stitch and Jay. Cassie kept a distance from Femi, demonstrating her extreme disapproval of Jay's decision. Jay and Stitch walked mostly in silence, concentrating on the effort needed to keep going in the soaring heat. The dry river bed meandered so much that Jay reckoned they must have walked ten times the shortest distance between the City and the hills. But it was necessary. If they were to find the source stone and have the power to retrieve it, then they would need to approach with stealth, not strength alone.

Cassie flopped down on the ground beneath the trees. Jay and Stitch caught up and did the same, before Femi arrived and leaned up against a tree, keeping himself a few feet from the three friends.

Despite being further from the source, and closer to the Readers' sink location, Jay sensed a greater level of Given power in the hills. It flowed down through the valleys like spring water. She considered the merits of pushing on, but decided they would be better to rest and recharge before taking their mission into the lair of the darkness. 'Let's camp the night here, build our strength for the morning,' she said.

'Not here,' Femi said. 'A little further in, beyond that tree line.' He pointed into the valley where the trees thickened and there would be greater cover.

Jay nodded and dragged herself to stand, not wanting to get used to resting until they reached their camp. She offered Cassie her hand, pulling her to stand. Cassie closed her eyes and swayed on her feet, exaggerating her fatigue for comic effect. Jay grabbed her around the waist and Cassie returned the hug, leaning down and resting her head on top of Jay's. Femi and Stitch headed into the valley. 'It'll be OK,' Jay whispered to Cassie. 'I think he's OK.' She nodded towards Femi.

'I trust your gut,' Cassie said. 'Just don't ask me to like him.'

Femi and Stitch found a place to camp. 'With a fire here,' Stitch said, 'the smoke will rise through this valley and dissipate before it reaches the hills. Anyone watching from a distance will see nothing.'

Cassie kicked at the dry soil and looked around the perimeter like she was checking for possible routes in for Readers, and escape routes in case it came to that.

'I'll help you look for wood,' she said, dumping her bag on the ground and bringing a look of surprise from Stitch.

In the valley, the trees brought a freshness and level of oxygen to the air that Jay hadn't felt since they arrived on Island 7. It reminded her of home, in the hills and countryside that was home to the hill forts and the Interland. She dumped her backpack and sat leaning against a tree. She looked up into the branches at the shiny, deep green leaves and green berries, wondering what kind of tree it was. She wished Alf was here to talk to.

'It's a Cape Ash,' said Femi, stepping closer to Jay and looking into the canopy above. He reached up and pulled at a leaf, drawing it closer to inspect, then brushed his hand over the light mottled grey bark of the trunk. 'Yes, an Ash tree.' He looked across the valley and pointed. 'There are more over there. They'll provide good cover.' He crouched next to Jay without sitting, as if asking for permission to stay a minute.

'What are those?' Jay nodded towards a string of trees filling the space between the bigger Ash trees.

Femi sat, holding his knees as he looked past Stitch and Cassie to the trees opposite. They too had a deep green colour to their leaves, but appeared to sparkle in the fading evening light. 'They are False Olives,' he said, smiling. 'They are common, but beautiful, yes?'

Their leaves shone in the warm glow of the remaining sun. Nestled between the taller Ash, they seemed modest, but sturdy and more than capable. 'Why false?' Jay asked.

'It's a harsh name perhaps,' said Femi. 'They look a bit like the olive tree, but they bear no fruit. No olives. Sometimes they are called the bastard olive. Even harsher, no?'

Jay laughed. 'They don't seem too bothered. They're doing pretty well by the looks of it.' She relaxed back against the tree, regarding Femi as he watched Stitch and Cassie build the fire.

'Tell me,' said Femi. 'What happened at the sink location on Island 8?' Jay shook her head gently, not wanting to get into a discussion on the darkness with Femi. But Femi continued, 'I don't mean the fight with Atta. I just mean what happened in the core. I'm interested in your connection to the Dark.'

Jay sighed, looking over as Stitch re-built the section of the fire that Cassie had done, the configuration of the lattice of branches apparently not to Stitch's exacting requirements. 'The truth is,' she said, turning to Femi, 'I don't really know what happened. I can't be confident...' She trailed off.

'Confident of what?' Femi pushed.

'I can't be sure the Dark won't eat me up from the inside. If I'm not in control, then it could put others at risk. With the Given power, I know what I can do, and I know I can keep us safe.'

'Until the darkness is stronger,' Femi said.

Jay thought again about Alf, and about Colson. She had spoken to Colson about the Event, and the residual dark energy Jay felt inside. He was still looking into it. He thought there must be something in the literature to give them a clue about the combination of light and Dark. Jay also wondered about Island 4, and the experience of that land in forcing out the darkness. There was still so much to learn.

'I've explored this connection,' said Femi. 'Like I said back at the cavern. I opened to it.'

'When I did that, I opened the channel for Atta to infiltrate our land.' Jay's tone was serious. She held Femi's eye. 'Do you understand? Someone died.'

'I'm sorry. That must be hard for you. But that's not what I mean. I explored the energy for myself. I didn't connect with Atta. Not sure I'd even be able to do that. But I can explore the dark energy, like anyone can, with a bit of effort.' Jay remained quiet. The silence grew. 'Let me explain,' Femi said, reaching for Jay's hand. She pulled it away. 'Sorry,' he said.

Stitch called over, 'Hey.' He smiled as he presented the fire, expertly crafted and smouldering on the inside. 'Come over,' he said as he delved in his bag. Jay joined Cassie and Stitch, leaving Femi back at the trees.

The light from the fire gradually replaced the dying glow from the sun. They ate some of their remaining food, Stitch sharing with Femi when he eventually joined them. Jay noticed that Cassie continued to avoid Femi, but Stitch was more friendly, engaging in conversation and accommodating Femi's thoughts on connections with the Dark power.

Femi caught Jay's eye from across the fire. 'You believe Tiago is alive?' he said.

Jay lowered her gaze, not wanting him to read her thoughts. 'We will see,' she said. 'Whether alive or dead, we will find him at the sink location.'

Femi shifted in his seat. 'The source stone is likely to have been destroyed,' he said. Then, quickly adding, 'Why would they keep it intact? They must know what it can do.'

He was right, but Jay couldn't allow herself to believe that the source stone had been destroyed. Without it, their mission was pointless. 'We will find it,' she said.

They talked into the night. Cassie dropped off to sleep first, then Femi not long after. Jay and Stitch lay on their sides by the fire, arm's reach from each other. The wood had burned down to embers, illuminating Stitch's face as they talked. 'A lot's happened,' Stitch said, almost absently, as he stared into the glowing embers.

'What do you mean?' said Jay.

'You remember at school when you were just learning what you could do?'

Jay laughed. 'Power can be dangerous in the hands of amateurs,' she said.

'I had nothing back then. I was convinced I'd never have any power. Don't suppose I have much, as it turns out.'

'Your power is crucial,' Jay said, her voice firm. She was annoyed by Stitch's negative attitude. She didn't like it when he was like this. He had a tendency to criticise himself that she found wasteful. 'Anyway, none of us had anything much back then.'

'Except you,' said Stitch. 'I'm pretty sure you knew more about what was in my head than I did most of the time.'

'Not sure I found very much,' Jay said with a smile.

'Can't argue with that,' said Stitch.

'I'd never knowingly read you without permission, of course,' said Jay, tongue in cheek.

'Yeah, rubbish,' laughed Stitch. 'Look, Jay, whatever happens here tomorrow, when we get to the sink room...'

'I know, I love you too, Stitch.'

'Yeah. Not what I was going to say, but, OK.'

They laughed. Cassie stirred.

'I was going to say, whatever happens, we need to communicate. You know what I mean?'

Jay knew what Stitch was saying. Their connection had been strong recently, as long as they were open with each other. But they still failed to communicate at times, and it made Jay sad, especially now that she had time to think about it. 'I know. You think I've been too stubborn, don't you?'

'No... never, not Jay, not stubborn.' He paused. 'Yes, stubborn as a donkey!'

'Mule.'

'What?'

'Stubborn as a mule.'

'Same thing,' said Stitch.

'I just can't allow the darkness to creep into my consciousness and distract, dilute...'

'That's what I mean,' said Stitch. 'We need to talk about this and agree, otherwise we'll be weak right when it matters the most. I'm not asking you to embrace the darkness no matter what. I'm asking you not to discount it out of hand.'

A howl in the distance startled Jay —an animal noise, but not any animal she was used to back home. Stitch rolled back onto his side so that he faced Jay. She studied his face. Dust and grime accentuated the creases in his skin and gave his hair a grey tint, making him look older than his twenty years. Rugged. Like he was growing into a man. His safety was as important to her as anything.

'At school,' Stitch said, returning to their previous conversation. 'We all knew that you had something brewing that was special. Alf knew too didn't he?'

'Alf knew a lot of stuff,' Jay said.

Stitch shifted onto his back so that he was looking directly up into the night sky. 'You miss him?'

'He was like a grandad to me. He taught me so much about the powers.'

'What would Alf think of Femi?' asked Stitch.

Jay thought for a minute. Alf used to be nervous of people with power he couldn't fully understand, like Femi's darkness. She wasn't sure what he'd make of Femi. When they'd first come across Flick, the Reader who had convinced Jay that she was on their side, and who turned out to be the one to orchestrate their near downfall, Alf had been cautious. 'I think he'd question our judgement in trusting someone with darkness. Especially after what Flick did.'

'This is a little different. Femi is Given. Flick was through and through a Reader and acting on their behalf.'

Jay agreed, but remained unsure. 'I'll talk to Femi tomorrow,' she said. 'Whatever happens, he's with us, so we deal with it.' Stitch's eyes were closed, but he smiled at Jay's agreement. 'Is that better?' she asked. 'Better communication?'

Stitch smiled again. 'You're getting there,' he said, his voice slowing as he dropped off to sleep.

Jay rolled her eyes. 'Night then, Stitch,' she said to no response, then rolled over onto her back, wide awake and ears pricked for sounds of approaching wild animals.

Chapter 8

When Jay woke, Stitch, Cassie, and Femi were already up, and the fire was burning once again, a small travel kettle perched above the flames on a makeshift wooden tripod.

'Coffee?' asked Stitch.

'You bet,' Jay croaked, sitting up and hugging her knees for warmth. The sun had not yet risen over the hills and the night's dew cooled her bones to the core. She looked around. Cassie was sitting under the Ash tree sorting through her bag. 'Where is he?' she asked.

'He said he was going up to the ridge to scout.' He looked up towards the ridge as if searching for him.

Jay took the tin mug of coffee from Stitch, warming her hands. The dark blue sky was cloudless, and early rays from the sun edged over the hills and washed through the valley.

Femi appeared through the trees and joined Jay and Stitch at the fire. He brushed some logs apart so that the fire would die down. 'We are closer than I thought,' he said. 'Safer if we don't attract any attention this morning. The smoke is more visible in these blue skies.'

'Did you see a route?' asked Stitch.

Femi nodded. 'A few hours trek if we take the route over the hills. Longer if we follow the valley. The hills will be safer, less likely to come across any Readers.'

Cassie joined them. 'Let's go then,' she said, slinging her rucksack on her back.

'I was thinking that Jay and I could go alone–' Femi started.

'No way,' said Cassie.

'Just to get some intelligence on the buildings through there, to confirm that the stone is there.'

'Why wouldn't it be there?' Cassie said.

Femi looked at Jay. She knew he thought the source stone was destroyed, and Jay couldn't be sure he was wrong. She wouldn't know until they got close enough for her to distinguish the energy of the source stone from the background noise of the Dark power. 'You think the stone is gone?' said Jay, looking into the fire.

'I don't know for sure,' he said. 'But we can scout ahead so we can better decide whether it's worth launching a full on grab for something that might be gone.'

'What about Tiago?' said Cassie. 'Is he worth fighting for?'

Femi looked away.

'We go together,' said Jay, ending the discussion.

As the group walked, Jay hung back to straighten her thoughts and pay attention to her powers. The energy from the source was weak, but there was power to be drawn from the immense physical mass of the hills and the ground beneath their feet.

As the energy flowed more freely in Jay's body, she sensed Angie's presence. She came to Jay through the power, crossing the vast physical distance between them as if it was nothing. Just 10-years-old, Angie's strength potential was clear. She was destined to be powerful. The number yet to emerge on her wrist would be high. She had wanted to come with Jay on this trip, but her parents wouldn't allow it. They said she was too young and vulnerable, and they were right, although Jay would have loved to have Angie alongside them. She brought a strength to Jay, and now, as her image came through, she felt the fizz of her little friend's energy course through her body.

'Hey, Angie,' Jay whispered into the breeze.

Whispers came back at Jay but they were the whispers of the power, not the voice of Angie. She opened herself to the energy by relaxing her muscles and opening her heart. The whispers became gradually clearer, and the voice transformed into that of Angie. 'Jay? Can you hear me?'

'I'm so pleased to hear you, little one.' Jay couldn't help but grin at the sound of Angie's voice. She'd missed it. They'd become so close through their combining of the power on Island 8. 'Wish you were here with me.'

'I am!' Angie said. 'Colson is here too.'

The mention of Colson saddened Jay. She couldn't think of him without thinking of Alf, who was lost to the Dark. 'Give him a hug for me,' Jay said.

'You seem a bit weird,' Angie said. 'Your signature in the power is muddled.'

'I'm strong. Everything here is bigger. The hills are taller, the mountains, the fields and valleys. So much potential for energy.'

'Are the Readers close?' asked Angie, her voice tentative.

'We think so. We're heading towards their camp through the hills.'

'You've been attacked?' said Angie. 'I can feel it. Is Tiago dead?'

'We'll find out soon enough. If he's alive, we'll get

him out. If they haven't destroyed the stone, we'll get it.'

'Colson says they can't destroy the source stone.'

'What do you mean?' Jay asked.

She sensed Angie smile. 'You know what he's like,' she said. 'He's been working day and night with the books. He thinks the stone can only be destroyed by a focus of energy of Given power, not Dark power.'

'Is he sure?'

'Hang on a minute,' Angie said, then waited while Colson said something to her. 'He says it's true. So it must be intact. You will find it. You must find it.' Angie's presence was strong. Jay felt her passion for the power of the Given, and for the survival of Island 7. Her positivity gave Jay a warm sense of hope.

'We'll find it,' said Jay. Angie's image faded a little as she slipped away from Jay's power. 'Stay a bit longer,' Jay pleaded, but Angie had already faded out of reach.

THE OTHERS LISTENED INTENTLY as Jay told them about Angie. Stitch smiled at the mention of their friend.

At the summit, they each crouched down

concealed from view behind a boulder. Jay slid in next to Stitch. 'What is it?'

Stitch nodded toward a small group of people in the depths of the valley, maybe four or five, standing alongside their Land Rover vehicles. Across the cutting in the hills, the route through the valley was cut off by a timber construction – a guarded gateway. 'Readers,' Jay said.

Femi straightened and scanned the hills to the north. 'We can skirt around them. Better if we stay under the radar.' He started along a narrow path that would take them away from the Readers, and on to a longer route.

Stitch followed. Cassie and Jay remained, taking a moment to observe the Readers. 'We could take them easily enough,' Cassie said.

'I agree. But I think Femi is right. We can't afford to give away the element of surprise. We need to keep hold of every advantage we can.' The Readers were smoking cigarettes and seemed to be settled in a well-worn operation. There were seats built into the rocks, with tables in front of them. Along the side of the valley was an open lean-to with a slatted roof structure for shade, and another closed structure that could be for sleeping quarters, or stores. This was no temporary facility.

Shouts from the distance startled Jay and Cassie.

Femi and Stitch were on the ground, pinned by Readers. As Jay and Cassie slid to a halt, the three standing Readers turned, immediately channelling their Dark energy towards Cassie and Jay. The power of all three combined was formidable, and Cassie took the initial blow, forcing her to the floor.

Jay subconsciously pegged all these Readers as power levels seven or eight and immediately began a counterattack, drawing the assault away from Cassie. But Jay struggled under the power of all three Readers. She sensed a level of recognition in them; they knew who she was, and they wouldn't give her a moment to break free of their grasp.

Cassie staggered to her feet, dispensing with the power. Time for a new tactic. She tackled the nearest Reader around the waist, piled in and forced him to the floor, knocking the wind from his lungs. She returned to her feet and swept the legs away from a second Reader, releasing the hold on Jay and allowing her to regain control. With her power restored, Jay took down the third Reader and turned her attention to Femi and Stitch. Femi had the upper hand with his two attackers, rendering one of them unconscious with his power alone, and the other subdued to a defensive position.

Jay had no time to be impressed by Femi, instead

turning her attention to Stitch. Cassie pulled one of the Readers from him and threw him to the floor with a force that was enough to knock him out as his head hit the hard surface. Cassie's power pulsed. She had fine-tuned her integration of physical strength and Given power. Keeping her distance, Jay entered the mind of the other Reader and squeezed hard until he flopped to the floor and Stitch could emerge.

Jay turned back to Femi, who continued to channel his attack on one of the Readers already unconscious. 'That's enough,' Jay said. 'He's out. That's enough!' Jay pulled at Femi's arm to drag him from his trance. He turned on her, his eyes blank, his fists clenched, but seeing Jay, he held himself back.

The darkness in Femi's eyes fizzled and died as he regained focus on Jay. 'What?' he said, his tone irritated.

Jay stepped back, unnerved. She didn't like being close to him.

Readers littered the ground like fallen trees. Her own power was depleted. The brief encounter had taken most of the reserves she had, and she felt vulnerable. Femi's dark edge wasn't helping to put her at ease. Stitch, too, looked damaged. He staggered a little and then leaned on Jay as he tried to stay on his feet. Cassie remained upbeat, like she'd drawn energy from the encounter. 'Let's move,' she said, her eyes flicking between the fallen Readers. 'We need to get away from here before more turn up.'

Jay and Stitch linked arms to help each other stay upright as they followed Cassie on the downward slope the other side of the summit. Jay pushed her mixed feelings around in her head about what she'd seen in Femi. The four of them had managed to take down a whole team of Readers, but her own contribution had been modest, and she was not at full strength by a long way. The effort of channelling the Given power in this land would take time to recover from. Stitch, too, was clearly drained.

Femi was an enigma. He channelled immense power; Given energy supplemented by a darkness. Jay couldn't shake the feeling of distrust. She explored that feeling for a moment and realised it was more than a simple uneasiness and distrust — it was fear. She saw what he was capable of, and it wasn't something she could contain without an effective connection to both the Given source and to Stitch, neither of which was strong in this land.

Stitch pulled Jay close, as if reading her thoughts. 'We'll be OK,' he said. 'The four of us are strong together.'

'I don't like it,' Jay said.

'Him?' He nodded at Femi, a few steps ahead of them. 'Is it him you don't like?'

'I literally can't read him. I don't know what he's thinking, so I can't be sure of his intentions.'

'This darkness,' he said. 'The element of it that's inside you, like it's inside him, it doesn't define you. You know that, right?'

Jay shrugged. 'It's whatever I allow it to be. I control my power, no-one else.'

'Exactly,' said Stitch. 'So you decide. It doesn't matter how your power is made up, or how you got it, even. What's important is how you react to it, how you use it, and the decisions you make.'

Jay rested her head on Stitch as they walked. She wanted to understand his perspective on the residual darkness within her, but she had a blocker, and Femi was not helping. The ambiguous nature of his energy did not make her inclined to explore or accept her own darkness. It made her resistant. 'I know,' she said. 'But I need to get it straight in my head so I can figure out what to do with it.'

Stitch stole a glance at Jay and she caught his expression. He feared what they were about to walk into. Jay did too.

IN LESS THAN AN HOUR, Femi and Cassie led them to a peak from which they could see the Readers' lair in the distance. It was like Jay remembered, but bigger.

The central structure was there, like a warehouse, and Jay knew that this held the rotating electro-source that drew the Dark power from the core – the sink facility. This was where they needed to take the source stone, if they could find it. Getting into the building would be easy enough. The challenge was how to do it without having to confront the full force of Atta. They wouldn't have the strength of force that they had back in their homeland, so their best option was a covert approach.

The landscape had changed since Jay saw it last. A small city had grown from the central source, like an expanding, multiplying organism. Buildings were just one or two storeys high. Some were clearly residences, others used for storage or some kind of industrial processes, judging by the emissions, and the stream of people moving between spaces in overalls.

'Are you getting anything?' asked Stitch. Any sense of the stone, or Tiago?'

Jay cleared her mind and drew in a deep breath. There were a multitude of power signals flowing and spiking from the buildings in the valley, and a strong pulsing energy from the sink facility, as she expected.

But there was nothing of the Given that she could discern.

Stitch shook his head. 'I got nothing either.' Femi stepped up next to Jay and pointed to the south side of the makeshift City. 'There. I'm getting something unusual from there.'

Jay followed the direction of his hand. The small building to which he referred was the very same one where she had been held by Atta the last time, and where the Island's level "C", Annika, Femi's mother, was killed in front of her. Images of the death flashed in her mind and she shuddered. 'Whatever is there is weak. If there's Given power, then it's not very healthy.'

'It could be shielded,' Femi said.

Cassie kicked at the ground. 'What choice do we have? We need to see for ourselves.' She peered over the ridge.

Jay stepped up to the edge to see if there was a way down. 'Too steep,' she said. 'We have to go around.'

Cassie walked the length of the cliff edge, evaluating the climb and plotting a route down. 'If we go around, it will be hours before we get down there.'

'She's right,' Femi said, joining Cassie.

'Here,' Cassie called. 'It's steep, but it looks possible.' She stepped down onto the next ledge, then shuffled sideways down a sandy bank baked hard by years of blazing heat.

Femi followed. 'It's OK,' he called back to Jay and Stitch.

The four of them edged slowly down the steep face of the hill. They were about half way down and making good progress when Femi slipped, landing on his backside and sliding perilously close to a ridge. Cassie turned and instinctively reached for him, her body leaning out close to the ridge so that she could use her weight to drag him back from the edge. As she did so, a section of the pathway crumbled and Cassie slipped.

She dropped Femi, who rolled away from the edge and out of danger, but Cassie couldn't regain her balance. More of the pathway crumbled and slipped down the slope. In a space of seconds, most of the pathway gave way and Cassie flowed down the slope with the tumbling stones and rocks. She made no noise but for a short, sharp inhale of breath as she disappeared from sight.

Jay's head spun with fear for her friend as she scrabbled on hands and knees to peer over the edge. She screamed Cassie's name, edging herself further over the ridge before Stitch took a hold of her leg and stopped her from following Cassie into the depths.

'She's there,' Femi said, pointing into the billowing

dust. As the dust cleared, Jay could see Cassie's body, motionless, about fifty feet below them.

She was on her back, her arm at an incongruous angle, not moving. Jay kicked her leg to free herself from Stitch's grasp. 'We need to get down there,' she said. She swung her legs around and edged herself down to the next ledge. Femi was one step ahead of her, on a parallel path.

Jay looked up at Stitch. Cassie would need his powers. 'I'm coming,' he said. 'Just take it slow. You'll help no-one if you end up on your back next to Cassie.'

Femi reached Cassie first, a minute before Jay. The bone in Cassie's forearm had breached the skin. Jay's stomach turned. She wobbled, then fell to her knees. She placed a hand on Cassie's head, stroking her hair. 'Cassie, it's me.' She leaned down to confirm that Cassie was breathing. Her chest rose and fell in a steady rhythm. Just as Stitch arrived at their side, Cassie opened her eyes. She screwed up her face in pain and tried to move. 'Stay still,' Jay said. 'Give it a minute. You fell a long way.'

Jay drew Stitch's eye and nodded towards Cassie's arm. He was already moving into position by Cassie's side. Cassie tried to move again, crying out in pain as she moved her arm. 'Still!' Jay said, firmer this time.

'My arm,' Cassie moaned, closing her eyes.

Femi looked shell-shocked, staring at Cassie's arm, not knowing what to do.

Stitch placed a hand on each side of Cassie's wound. She cried out again and Jay tried to calm her, stroking her head. 'It's OK. Stitch is going to do some work on your arm.'

'What's wrong with it?' Cassie tried to move to see her arm but Jay insisted she remain still.

Stitch closed his eyes and steadied his breathing. Jay read his thoughts as he channelled power from inside himself through to his hands. There were images of Thabisa in Stitch's head as he tried to connect with her over distance, to combine his own healing power with that of Thabisa.

Something was happening. A glow emitted from beneath Stitch's hands. Femi's eyes widened so Jay knew he saw it too. Jay felt a forceful presence of Thabisa, coming to support Stitch through the power as he healed. The glow intensified and after a minute or two, subsided. Stitch eventually opened his eyes.

Cassie remained quiet, her eyes closed. Stitch peeled back his hands and Femi gasped. The breach of the skin had disappeared, as if the bone had shifted back into place and the skin closed. Stitch seemed as surprised as Femi and Jay at how effectively he had applied healing. Jay had seen Stitch affect healing before, and had even been the beneficiary. But this was the next level.

'Well done,' Jay said, reaching to put a hand on Stitch's arm.

Stitch was drained – pleased and shocked with what he'd achieved, but drained. 'She's got other injuries. I can feel it,' he said.

'We need to move from here,' Femi said, drawing Jay's attention to their location. There was a direct line of sight to the Reader City further below them in the valley. 'Can we move her?'

Jay nodded. 'We have no choice. See if there's somewhere we can shelter.' Femi made off around the corner of the cliff face. Jay stroked Cassie's hair again, and she opened her eyes. 'How are you doing?' Jay said.

'Fine. Did he...' Cassie started, looking at Stitch and then down to her arm. She stroked the skin and winced with pain.

'Still bad?' Stitch asked.

'Sore. But nothing like it was five minutes ago. Is this down to you?' Stitch smiled and Cassie gave him a nod of thanks.

'You're welcome,' Stitch said. 'Do you have pain anywhere else?'

'Everywhere,' Cassie said. Stitch stood and reached

out a hand for Cassie. Jay stood too, positioning herself to take Cassie's weight as she leaned into her. With Stitch on one side and Jay on the other, Cassie moved gingerly.

Femi came running back to them. 'Not much further. There's good shelter ahead, out of the sun and out of sight. We can rest.'

'No time to rest,' said Cassie.

'We're going to rest,' said Jay.

The shelter was a shallow cave in the face of the cliff, deep enough to shelter but not so deep as to be useful to any other wildlife. Jay and Stitch lowered Cassie onto a rock, where she pulled her arm into her body to cradle it. She stretched out her leg and Jay saw she had another wound – a cut the length of her shin that showed through a rip in her trousers. She knelt down to look.

'It's nothing,' said Cassie.

The cut was deep, and Cassie's shoe was saturated in her blood. Cassie was shivering, despite it being over thirty degrees in the shade. 'You've had a big shock, Cassie. You need to just rest a minute.' She looked at Stitch. 'Can you do more?'

'I need to recharge.'

'What if I help?' she said.

'And me,' said Femi.

Stitch considered for a moment, then nodded.

'Worth a try.' He crouched next to Cassie, and she leaned back against the rocks, her eyelids drooping.

Femi crouched next to him. 'What do I need to do?' he said.

'You and Jay each put a hand on top of mine. Don't overthink it, just be open in your body and mind. Let me do the work.' With this, Stitch placed a hand on Cassie's lower leg, and another just below the knee. Cassie groaned and slumped back in her seat. Jay put a hand on one of Stitch's, and Femi did the same with Stitch's other hand.

A surge of energy flowed from the rocks and the ground into Stitch and through to Cassie. Jay's own hand grew warm on top of Stitch's. Gathering herself, she opened to the energy to try to support the focus of power. Femi shifted his position so that he had one hand touching the wall of the cave and the other pressed firmly on top of Stitch's. A spark of light - Given energy - flowed through the wall and into Femi. His eyes closed. A wisp of darkness entwined with the light and Jay felt a bolt of power, like a surge of electricity.

Jay rocked in her position, having to concentrate on keeping her hand on Stitch's. She closed her eyes. The flow of energy took on a changing signature, an evolving feel. Her own darkness, buried deep inside her for so long, became entangled in the stream of power that flowed through Femi and Stitch. It rose through her body and mixed with the Given energy as the four of them became a single entity of power.

The silence that came after reflected the confusion in Jay's mind, and, she guessed, in the others too. Cassie lay on her back, eyes closed and chest moving steadily with her deep breaths. Stitch came to and leaned over Cassie to check on her. Jay looked at Femi and he looked away, refusing to make eye contact.

'She's OK,' Stitch said. He examined her leg. 'It's healed over. She lost a lot of blood. I don't know if she'll be able to continue. Not for a day or so.'

Jay looked at Femi. 'What did you do?' Her tone was accusatory.

He nodded towards Cassie. 'We did it together. It worked. Look!' He stood and turned away.

Jay was consumed by unfocused anger. What she felt was fear. You opened me up,' she said.

'I didn't intend to. It just happened,' he said without turning around.

'That makes it even worse,' said Jay.

Stitch frowned. 'What are you two talking about?'

'Him,' Jay said with bitterness. 'He didn't just use Given power just now with Cassie. He drew on the darkness.'

Stitch didn't look surprised. 'The important thing is it worked. We've stopped the bleeding.'

'You don't understand. It wasn't just his darkness. He tapped into me.' Jay sensed no feelings of guilt coming from Femi. He believed what he did was justified. Jay's voice trembled with anger as she spoke. 'It doesn't matter what you believe about the darkness, or what you think I should be doing. It's not your decision.' Jay could still feel the after-effects of the darkness running through her body. It was like Femi had unleashed a poison to seep into her bloodstream from where it had previously lain dormant, from where she'd suppressed it within herself.

Femi turned around. 'Look at Cassie. Open your eyes, Jay, instead of just thinking about yourself.'

Jay looked at Stitch for support, but he avoided her eye. 'Stitch. We talked about this. You said we needed to open up our communication if we are to beat the darkness down there in the valley. This, whatever is happening here, is not opening up our communication. This is not working together.'

'Look...' Femi started, his tone conciliatory.

Jay cut him off. 'If you ever do anything like that again,' she stepped closer to him.

He raised his hands in defence. 'OK. I get it.'

Cassie stirred. Stitch went to her. The tension broke a little as Jay joined Stitch at Cassie's side. Stitch helped her to sit up and handed her a bottle of water. Cassie took a sip and then closed her eyes.

'She's not going anywhere anytime soon,' said Stitch.

Twice Cassie attempted to stand, insisting that she would be OK and that she could come. Both times she was dizzy and had to sit back down.

'Do we wait until she's strong enough?' Jay asked Stitch.

Before Stitch could answer, Femi piped up. 'No time. And, besides, we don't have supplies, food, nothing. We can't just sit here.'

'He's right,' said Stitch. 'Cassie is comfortable here. She has shade. We can pick her up on our way back out.'

'We don't know what we will face down there,' said Jay. 'We don't know what our exit plan is.'

'We have no choice,' said Femi, his tone frustrated. Jay ground her teeth. She knew Femi was right. They didn't have time to waste, but she hated to admit it.

'OK,' said Jay. She leaned down to Cassie and adjusted her makeshift pillow to get comfortable. 'We'll be back. A few hours, OK?' Cassie nodded, resigned now to the fact she would be of no use to them.

Jay grabbed her rucksack and flung it on her back. 'Let's do it then,' she said, still unable to look at Femi. She stormed from the cave as Stitch and Femi gathered their things.

Stepping out onto the ledge, Jay steadied herself

with a hand on a tree, its trunk leaning precariously and its roots poking out from the cliff face below, reaching to re-root itself. The sprawling city of darkness in the flat valley below oozed confidence, like nothing could touch it, nothing could deflect it from its inevitable control of Island 7. But in their hearts, they believed there was still a chance. They had to believe this. They had to keep going.

Chapter 9

The three Given took a route around the edge of the City, keeping a few hundred feet outside its perimeter fence at all times. Their target destination was at the southern edge, close enough to the perimeter that they would only need to breach the boundary when they were almost there.

As they neared the southern edge, Femi drew alongside Jay. 'What's the plan?' he asked, happy to hand Jay the lead for the first time.

'In my experience, the only way in is to walk straight through the front door.'

They reached a six-foot-high chain-link fence and stopped. Stitch caught them up and Jay led him and Femi back into the bushes for cover. 'The fence is weak, clearly for show more than keeping people out,

Femi said. 'We can pull it away from the post over there.' He pointed.

'Agreed,' said Jay. 'Then we head straight for the door. The route is clear, and if we prime our power first, we'll be ready for whatever we meet. If we have the stone, we take cover, re-group, and then go again. Agreed?'

Stitch craned his neck to see the route from the fence to the front steps of the building they hoped contained Tiago and the stone. 'Why are there no guards?'

They were all thinking the same thing. 'We need to check it out, anyway. Maybe it is there but they've become over confident. They don't expect an attack. If it's not there, then we retreat and think again. Keep your senses open to see if you can pick up any sense of the stone, or of Tiago.'

Jay tore at the fence. It came away from the post and she held it back so that Stitch and Femi could crawl through. Femi then held it for Jay to squeeze under. Her heart raced now that they'd breached the boundary. A weak sense of Given power came from the building ahead and she dared to hope.

And then a second, more powerful and sickly familiar feeling washed over Jay. She stopped dead in her tracks. 'Atta,' said Jay. Femi nodded. He felt it too. Stitch scanned the open area in front of the buildings like he expected Atta to appear. 'Keep going. We're exposed here.'

Femi and Stitch led the way up the steps to the front door, with Jay keeping watch over their approach. There were Readers milling around, passing between buildings. None of them gave more than a glance in their direction as Jay continued to shield. A Reader appeared from the nearest building and Jay held her breath. He glanced at Jay, then looked away, only to look a second time. Jay doubled her focus on shielding, hoping not to have to fight. Then the Reader nodded before moving on his way. Jay breathed again.

Femi closed his hand around the door handle.

'There's energy coming from inside,' said Jay.

They clasped hands in a stack, taking a moment to build their energy. When they felt it flow, a tingling that fizzed through their muscles into their fingertips, Jay whispered, 'One... two... three.'

Femi flung open the door and they piled into the building, ready to fight.

The room was empty.

A wooden table stood at the far end, a small crate on top. Jay sensed Tiago, a residual energy, and knew immediately that she had been right. He was dead. Whatever remained of him was in the crate.

Femi strode over to the crate and ripped off its lid without hesitation. Inside were two metal cylinders.

'Ashes,' said Femi, carefully lifting one of the containers in both hands.

Jay picked up the other. It was heavy, and she too had to use both hands. 'Annika,' she said, glancing at Femi. Annika, Tiago's connected C, was Femi's mother. Atta had killed her in front of Jay the last time she was there.

Femi read Jay's thoughts. 'You are the one who saw her die.' His expression hardened 'Why couldn't you save her?'

'I was in no place to help, even myself. Atta was too strong.' Femi stood fast in front of Jay, then turned away, back to the container in his hand. They were quiet for a moment.

Femi studied Tiago's metal container as if it had something written on it. Femi and Tiago would have been close, perhaps as close to family as Femi had left on Island 7 after his mother died. 'I'm so sorry,' Jay said.

The container in Jay's hand emitted a sense of Annika. She pictured her pleading eyes as Atta reduced her to ashes. As her world's 8C, and Stitch her connected C, they were far from invincible.

'No sign of the source stone,' said Stitch, pacing the perimeter of the inside of the hut, scouring the shelves and cupboards. Jay replaced Annika's ashes in the wooden crate. She put a hand on Femi and startled him from his inner thoughts. He placed Tiago's remains back next to Annika's.

Stitch opened the door to check the coast was clear. They crept back to the bigger building next door and Femi strode in without hesitation.

A wall of metal bars at the back marked the opening to the prison cell where Jay had seen Annika breathe her final breath. The door to the cell was open.

Femi called back from where he was examining the debris in the cell. 'It was here. The stone was here, in this crate.'

Jay felt the power straightaway. It was undeniable. A powerful energy signal remained, like a residue inside the crate. 'They've taken it,' said Stitch.

'Or destroyed it,' said Femi, voicing their worst fears.

'Colson said that the Readers cannot destroy the stone, remember? He said Dark power can never destroy the source. The only power that can destroy the source stone is Given power.'

'No Given will destroy the stone,' said Stitch.

'Let's not forget what happened the last time we thought we were protected from the darkness,' said Jay, referring to their betrayal by a Reader, Flick, who tricked them into allowing her to assume the power of the Given and open a channel for the Dark to move into their homeland.

Stitch nodded. 'But surely...' he trailed off.

Femi crouched near the middle of the cell, running the dust through his fingers. 'She died here,' he whispered, bowing his head and collecting a handful of the dust, releasing it through his fingers.

'I'm sorry,' said Jay.

Femi did not look up but continued to stare into the dust in his hand.

Without warning, the door of the building flung open, as if pushed by a gust of wind, and slammed against the inside wall. Jay raised her defences and stepped back from the entrance. Femi stood, and Stitch positioned to the side of Jay.

Atta stepped through the doorway.

Femi attacked immediately, without thinking. Atta raised a hand as if it was a nuisance to do so, flinging Femi back against the wall inside the cell. He fell to the floor and remained motionless. Stitch and Jay took a further step back. The sight of Atta sent spears of adrenaline through Jay's body. She froze; her overriding terror was that Atta could use her to get to the people she loved. He had done it before. He used her to get to Alf, channelling his power through Jay's own power to destroy her friend and mentor.

Readers poured into the room behind Atta, some with guns, most without. Jay and Stitch raised their hands in a defensive gesture. They would not be able to fight against these odds. Femi remained crumpled, unconscious on the floor.

'Jay is correct,' Atta said, walking over to Femi and dragging him up by his collar and slamming him back against the wall. He slid back down and Atta dragged him up by his hair. Femi regained consciousness and screamed in pain as Atta slammed him against the wall once more. This time Femi remained upright as Atta required of him. 'Your source stone was here.'

Jay's anger bubbled. The Darkness that flowed within her subdued her power. It was as if her arms were glued to her sides, and her power trapped inside her body.

'Oh, don't worry. We're keeping your little stone safe, somewhere you'll never find it.'

'In there,' Atta said, waving Jay and Stitch towards the cell where Femi rested against the wall, his head lolling as he drifted in and out of consciousness. With a force of dark power at their heels, Jay and Stitch stumbled into the cell. The door swung closed behind them and locked with a thud.

Jay stepped back from the bars, as far away from Atta as possible. He had killed Alf by reaching inside Jay with his power, from close range. She could not allow herself to be the pathway for the death of anyone else. Her heart swelled as she thought of her dad, her mum, and of Sammy. Or was it Angie he wanted? Angie would be a big future threat to the Dark. She pushed the thoughts from her mind and shielded herself from Atta's digging.

'Why have you kept their ashes?' As Jay spoke, she dug, but read nothing in his mind. His defences were strong.

Atta nodded. 'A trophy, I suppose,' he said, looking at Jay. 'You will join them soon enough.'

Jay ignored the threat. 'Seems the action of the source stone inside the core was not enough to finish you, just enough to expel you.'

'I won't be making the same mistake again. Once is fair enough. Some would say you were lucky, but I think it was a fair fight. You won fair and square. A second time would be unforgivable, negligent even. Yet here you are?'

'We have no plans to make this easy for you.'

Atta laughed. 'You impress me, I must admit. But sadly, you can't stop us this time. We have the source stone.'

Vulnerability flickered in Atta and Jay zoomed in on it. 'What good is that if you can't destroy it?' When his eyes snapped up to meet hers, it was confirmed. She was right. 'As long as it exists, the Given have a chance of finding it, and you will never be safe here. This will never be your land.'

Streams of his darkness and anger flowed around his body. Stitch nudged Jay to stop provoking him.

Atta approached the bars. Jay squeezed herself hard against the back wall. She felt the waves of his power: angry, aching to attack. 'You're right,' he said, his voice a little raspy, almost a whisper. Then, focused once more, he said, 'We can't destroy the source stone in its current form.' He paused for a reaction.

'Current form?' Stitch said.

Atta seemed to notice Stitch for the first time and smiled. 'Yes. But after we reduce it, I don't expect a problem.'

'You can't,' said Stitch.

'Everything is vulnerable. Every stone has its crack.' Atta's expression darkened, the lines on his face deepening as a half-smile twisted into something more sinister. Jay felt the depth of his madness, not for the first time. She became momentarily sucked into the whirlpool of his mind and had to catch her breath. She shook her head clear, but a bitter taste resided in her mouth. Images of his thoughts flashed behind her eyes. There was more to his plans than he was letting on.

'How?' Stitch asked, his tone less enthusiastic as Atta started to enjoy himself.

'It won't matter to you,' Atta said, turning from

Stitch and locking eyes with Jay once more, closing off his mind as he did so. 'Funny,' said Atta. 'The weakening of the power of the Given in this land has been easier than others. There's been almost no resistance. He turned to one of the Readers and nodded, sparking their exit from the building.

Jay looked at Atta and caught a smug expression as he turned to leave. 'Hey,' Jay called after him. 'So this is it. You finish this as a coward?'

Atta choked a laugh. 'There's more than enough time to finish this. You won't be alone here for long. As soon as we are done, I'll be back to reduce you to dust, like your friends.' He stepped back towards the bars and Jay recoiled. 'Or you could let me in again if you like,' he said. 'Like last time. We could see how much resistance your family can muster if you give me a channel?'

'Leave me alone,' Jay said, her hands trembling.

'Alf was not so easy. Took me a little while to get through to him. Did you tell the others how his death was your fault?' He looked at Stitch. 'What about Sammy?' He reached through the bars as though to stroke Jay's face but she shrunk away. 'Perhaps you can also let me have Sammy. What would your dad say then? If the big sister was the cause of little Sammy's sudden and unexpected death?'

Atta was capable of getting to any of Jay's loved

ones. He'd shown it before. She was not strong enough to resist him.

'Thought as much,' Atta said. 'So now you will be contained here, in this cell. And then, when we have what we need, we can make sure you have a nice souvenir container like your friends, Tiago and Annika. There's some poetry in it don't you think? The level 8C and her connected C from Island 8 meeting the same end, in the same place, as their counterparts here on Island 7. And the boy is just a bonus.' Femi blanched white with fear.

Atta ushered the Readers from the room. Before exiting, he said, 'We won't be sparing the others,' he said. 'We know the location of your underground.' Then he turned and left.

THE WOODEN DOOR slammed closed behind Atta, and they were alone.

'I saw something,' said Jay, trying to grasp at the pictures in her head from Atta's thoughts.

'What was it?' asked Stitch.

Jay frowned and rubbed her forehead. 'I can't–'

'Look,' Femi said, an urgency in his tone. He stamped on the floor of the cell in the far corner.

'What?' said Stitch.

'Listen,' he said, stamping his foot. 'The echo. There's a void underneath. There are fractures in the rock mass in Kaapstown.'

'Interesting,' said Stitch. 'But we have more important things to talk about right now than geology.'

Femi scraped around the edge of the concrete slab that formed the floor of the cell, stamping his feet. Where the floor met the far wall, he prised his fingers around the slab. He grunted. The slab made no signs of movement.

'Here,' said Jay, reaching through the cell bars to a chair. She stretched, her fingers just scraping the leg of the chair but unable to grasp it. She pushed once more and her fingers curled around the metal chair leg. She pulled it towards herself and levered one of the legs against the bars until it broke free.

Femi took the chair leg and went back to work on the concrete slab. With all three of them leaning on the chair leg, the slab moved a little. 'Again,' said Femi.

With a loud crack, a small section of the concrete broke away under the force of the lever. Femi scraped with his hands. He lay on his front and peered through the gap. 'I was right. And it's huge,' he said. 'This is our way out.'

They went to work on the concrete, chipping it away in small sections, with the occasional larger piece edging free. After a few minutes, there was enough space for each of them to crawl through.

They had to duck down in the space below the cell. 'Look.' Jay pointed towards a passageway through a fissure in the rock.

'How do we know it's not a dead end?' said Stitch.

'We don't,' said Jay. 'But what choice do we have? We need to get clear before anyone realises we're not here.'

Together, they made their way through to the wide diagonal crack in the rock that opened up a space big enough for them to slide into a wider passageway. It stretched at an incline for as far as Jay could see. In the distance, a crack of light penetrated the passageway.

'Follow me,' Jay said, leading the way through the rocks, careful not to lose her footing. The rock surface was hard and jagged, not like the softer mud-stone on the surface. A fall on these rocks would do damage that might be difficult to survive in a location way beneath the surface, especially with Readers on their trail.

For nearly twenty minutes they scrabbled through the rocks and still there was no sign of a route to the surface. The shards of light that penetrated all came through cracks far too small for them to negotiate, so they could do nothing but keep moving. There were no signs of anyone following them, and Jay had no sense that there were Readers anywhere close.

'They must know about these passages?' Stitch said.

'They're not man made and they're not from here, so probably not. At least we get a head start.'

'Which direction are we heading?' Stitch asked. 'For all we know, we might be heading deeper into their City?'

'South or East,' Femi said. 'We've already passed under the perimeter fence, I felt it.'

Jay kept on making her way through the rocks, feeling her way in the dark and by her senses. She was exhausted and breathing heavily, but determined not to stop and rest until she could see a way out to the surface. They had to get to Cassie, and get warning back to the underground. Then they would have to figure out what Atta was planning, and the meaning behind the images Jay had seen in his head.

Chapter 10

Just as Jay was losing hope, they turned a corner in the underground passageway and light poured in from above. They blinked as their eyes adjusted. Jay scanned the top of the shaft for any signs of movement before stepping into the light. 'Looks clear. An easy enough climb.'

'Careful at the top,' said Femi. 'We don't know how close we are to their camp. They are probably searching for us by now.'

Jay nodded and tightened the straps on her rucksack before pushing herself up the rock face. After the first two footholds, which were a stretch, the going was good. The rock was fractured with discontinuities that provided perfect ledges for climbing. She looked over her shoulder and saw Stitch a few feet below, taking the same route. Femi was across the other side of the opening, finding his own way to the top. Jay paused a moment and watched as he stretched for impossible handholds. He was a climber for sure, and he was enjoying himself as he overtook Stitch to be first to the top.

They emerged into the baking sunlight. Jay and Femi tentatively raising their heads above ground as they scanned their surroundings. They were at least two hundred feet from the perimeter fence, further than Jay had thought. And there was cover of boulders and bushes to enable them to climb out unseen.

Jay pulled herself up and onto her back, rolling away from the hole and to a safe location behind a string of rocks. As soon as she was clear, she settled to prepare herself for sending communication back to Thabisa in the underground cavern. If Atta was telling the truth, then the Readers might already be on their way there.

'What are you doing?' Stitch said as he bumped up next to Jay.

'Getting warning to Thabisa.' Jay closed her eyes and connected with the power of the Given that flowed from the ground. The whispers were weak, the power subdued by the nearby dominant Dark energy. Stitch put a hand on Jay's arm and she felt a widening of the channel to the Given energy. Her chest tingled.

Thabisa's image came to her. 'You need to leave,' Jay said.

'And go where?' said Thabisa. 'What about Tiago?' Thabisa's voice was soft, almost a whisper. Jay took a breath, unsure how to let Thabisa know Tiago was dead, that he'd not survived the attack at the lake. Her hesitation was enough. 'He's dead,' Thabisa said. 'I think I knew. Deep down.'

'I'm sorry,' said Jay. 'But there's more. You must listen now. We think they have your location, and they could be on their way.'

'What about the source stone?' Thabisa asked.

'We haven't found it yet. But we haven't given up. We saw Atta. We got away, but he's planning something—'

'What?' Thabisa's tone was less patient.

'I think he's trying to weaken the power of the stone so they can destroy it. But please—'

'Then we stay here,' Thabisa interrupted.

'Readers will come.'

'And we will defend. We cannot desert this place until you have exhausted all efforts to get the source stone into the core. You will need the energy from here.'

'Then please prepare. Protect yourselves.'

'We will be ready.'

'We need to head up into the hills. I feel it. We may call on your support.'

'We will be here.' Thabisa's image wavered, and Jay allowed the communication to fade.

Stitch let go of Jay's arm. 'She's stubborn,' he said.

'She's got fight in her. She won't let her husband's death count for nothing.' What Jay didn't voice was her fear. Thabisa's stubbornness could lead to mass murder. The remaining Given on the island were outnumbered.

'I feel it too,' said Stitch.

'What?'

'The hills,' he said. 'The draw is strong. I just hope it's a positive draw, not another trap.'

'We have no choice.'

Femi nudged into Jay. 'We should leave,' he said, peering above the rocks towards the fence. He turned and pointed into the hills to the east. 'That way?'

'To Cassie first,' said Jay with a nod.

Femi made a dash across open land to the next group of rocks, then pressed on into the hills. Jay nudged Stitch to follow Femi, then took a last look at the Readers' camp before following the others into the hills.

In under half an hour, they were back on the ridge that led around to the cave where they left Cassie. Jay was the first to enter, heading straight for the resting place where she'd last seen her friend.

The blood stained rocks where Stitch had healed Cassie's leg wound were baked in sun, but there was no sign of her, or her things. Stitch and Femi spread out to search every corner of the shallow cave but it was empty. 'Anything?' called Jay, hopefully.

'Nothing,' replied Stitch.

'You think she came down to find us...?' Jay said, her words trailing off as she contemplated the possibility that Cassie had made her way into the Readers' City to find them, to help them.

'Surely not,' Stitch said.

'Where else would she go?'

Femi crouched near where Cassie had rested. 'Readers came,' he said. 'There are more footprints than just ours.'

Jay and Stitch tried to see what Femi was looking at but there was little more than a random array of markings in the dust. 'You think she ran?' Jay asked.

Femi stood. 'Whatever happened, it doesn't look like there was much of a fight.'

Jay kicked at the wall. Why didn't she sense Cassie was in trouble? She had been too distant from her friend. This should never have happened. Stitch put a hand on her arm. 'She'll be OK. You know Cassie. She knows the Reader signals too well. She would have been long gone by the time they walked in here.'

'I don't know,' Jay said. 'When we left her, she was barely conscious.' She kicked herself for allowing the darkness to rise in her, for not keeping true to the energy of the Given, the only energy she could truly trust. It was the Given energy that would win their battle with the darkness. Jay appealed directly to Stitch. 'We need to build the energy of the Given if we are to find the stone and figure out what Atta is up to. Thabisa will help us, but we need to keep the darkness from filtering through, diluting.'

'I understand,' said Stitch.

'It's not that simple,' said Femi, stepping into the middle of the discussion. 'You felt it,' he said to Jay. 'Tell me you didn't,' he said, challenging.

'It doesn't matter what I felt. We only get one go at this. We are Given, and we need to maximise the power we can draw.'

Jay walked away, out of the cave and back to the ridge where she could breathe again. Concealing herself in the trees, she looked down into the valley of the City of Readers. The building from which they had escaped was visible. There was no sign of Readers running through the streets, sirens wailing. Cassie came into her mind and she focused on her image, trying to force the energy to locate her, give her a sign that she was alive. She felt sick at the thought of Cassie taken again by Readers. She had vowed not to let this happen again, not after the last time when they lost Cassie's longtime friend Reuben, and they nearly lost Cassie.

She turned back to the cave where Stitch and Femi emerged. 'Let's go,' she said, unable to hide the frustration and anger in her voice.

'Where?' Femi called after her as she strode on through the trees and onto the path.

'Up into the hills,' she said. 'We need to plot a route through to the valleys where the unnamed river flows.'

RESTING in the shade of a tree, Jay crouched, waiting for the others to catch up. Femi arrived first. 'You set quite a pace,' he said.

Jay remained silent, turning Atta's images over in her mind.

'What is it?' Femi asked.

Stitch joined them, flopping down to lean up against the tree, out of breath.

'I saw something in Atta's thoughts back at their camp. But it made no sense. It wasn't clear.'

'Something to do with the river?' asked Stitch, as if he knew.

'Yes!' said Jay, turning to him. 'You saw it too?'

Stitch shook his head. 'I see it in you, not him.'

'Construction,' said Jay. 'I think they're building something near the river, or *in* the river.'

'A bridge?' said Femi.

Jay shook her head. 'I don't know. Maybe. Something like that.'

'So what?' said Femi.

'A dam!' shouted Stitch, standing to join Jay and Femi. 'They're building a dam across the unnamed river.'

Jay nodded. The images came into greater focus in her mind and she knew Stitch was right. 'Of course. It makes sense. If they dam the river, the Given power will be stifled, weakened. And they might reduce it enough to –'

'Destroy the source stone,' Femi said.

'You think they've built it already?' said Stitch.

'I don't know,' said Jay. 'But we need to find it. We have to stop them from completing it.'

Stitch paced. 'How are we supposed to know where on the river they're building it? It could be anywhere.'

Femi pulled a map from his rucksack. Stitch crouched with him and he followed the path of the unnamed river along its most likely trajectory – back through the valleys and up towards the peaks of the hills and mountains of Kaapstown.

Jay watched as Femi and Stitch debated the likely paths, but her focus remained on opening up her senses. If they were to be sure, she would need to use all of her perceptive powers. The path of the river itself she could reasonably feel, albeit the river flowed for some of its length underground. The difficulty was predicting exactly where the Readers would choose to dam the river. If they were to get there quickly, they would need to waste no time in figuring out the dam's position. This is where Stitch's skills of analysis and deduction might come in handy.

'Where's the best location for the dam?' Jay asked.

Stitch didn't look up, but continued to study the map. 'Two possible places. One out in the open, across the valley... here.' He pointed to a place on the map deep in the hills. 'The other is an underground cavern. If they decide to divert the river by changing the paths of the underground channels, then they would most likely choose here.' He pointed to a location further down, back towards the City.

'There are probably ten miles between those places. We can't go to both. We have to choose,' said Jay. Stitch nodded.

'Femi? Any feel for it?' He shook his head.

Jay looked up to the sky and took a breath. 'We head to the valley. If they are serious about it, they will need to confirm the river is diverted by the dam. If it's underground, it could end up heading off on a pathway they can't see. They won't risk that.'

'Valley it is,' Stitch said, folding the map and handing it to Femi.

'Agreed,' said Femi, packing the map away and moving off. They were a good five-mile walk from the location Stitch pointed out, and under the afternoon heat of the Kaapstown sun, they wouldn't be able to move quickly.

They trekked along the ridge, a good few hundred feet above the floor of the valley. Below them, streams and springs burst from the rock face and poured down into the depths as if hunting for the main river. Jay paused a moment and reached down to a spring, taking the cool water into her hands and to her lips. The energy in the natural spring was reassuring. There was power remaining in the hills. Whatever the Readers did, there would be a chance of revival of the environment.

A noise caught Jay's attention – voices in the distance. The wind high up in the hills whistled around the rocks overhanging the valley. They backed into the rock wall, keeping out of sight.

'How far from the site are we?' Jay said, thinking

that whoever was nearby, they must be Readers. And, if there are Readers, they must be there for a reason.

'Still a couple of miles out,' said Stitch. 'There's nowhere suitable for a dam here. The river doesn't pass through this section.

'Well there's someone here,' Jay said, although she could no longer hear the voices and questioned herself over whether it could have been the wind. She peered around the side of the hill towards the source of the sound. As she stepped out from the cover of the cliff and onto the pathway, a shot rang out. A bullet pinged off the rocks just a few feet from where she stood.

Jay threw herself back up against the cliff.

Stitch pulled her in. 'What the...' he stuttered.

'Readers,' said Femi. 'The worst kind. The ones with guns.'

'Did you see how many?' asked Stitch.

Jay shook her head, gathering her nerves. Femi motioned he would double back the way they came. 'We will have to fight,' he whispered. 'You two wait thirty seconds and then go. I'll come at them from the back.'

Jay nodded and edged forward. Her fear transitioned to anger. She was ready for a fight. 'Stitch, follow my lead. We'll need to work together.'

'What have you got in mind?'

'Power,' said Jay. 'Let's use it like we know we can. Pure and simple.'

Stitch nodded and followed close behind Jay as she edged around the path at the base of the cliff. Through a gap in the overhanging trees above them, there was movement. Three, maybe four people stalking the ridge. They were no more than fifty feet up. Femi would be manoeuvring around behind them already. She opened her senses to see what intelligence she could gather. Stitch put a gentle hand on her arm, and it was clear there were six of them, not four. And Femi was close. He was ready.

'Ready?' said Jay, speaking both to Stitch and also to Femi. For Femi, the message was that they would hold until he was also ready to go, so they could attack at the same time. Stitch responded positively without speaking aloud. They agreed to use the power to weaken the Readers as much as possible without exposing themselves to the risk of getting shot. At least until they were confident they could overcome.

A noise from above, and a pulse of energy through the air. Femi had launched his assault.

Jay and Stitch delved deep into the energy of the land, drawing too from the Given power of the nearby watercourses. The energy of the unnamed river, closer than they'd thought, poured into Jay.

The group of readers had split. Two ran into the

hills, the other four were down. Femi emerged from the trees as Jay and Stitch made their way up towards him, their power firmly directed at the four remaining Readers on the ground. The power of the Given was strong. Femi too joined with Jay and Stitch's attack, adjusting his frequency so that the three were aligned. By the time Jay and Stitch reached Femi, stood over the Readers. All four were unconscious and showing no signs of movement.

'That's enough,' said Jay.

Femi backed off and looked up into the distance where the other two Readers made their escape. 'Where are they headed?' Femi said with an air of amusement. They were running towards the higher peaks, not in the direction of the dam, or at least where they believed the dam to be.

'You think we have it wrong?' said Stitch.

'It doesn't matter. Let's keep our focus on the dam,' said Jay. 'We have no choice, it's our best bet.'

They moved off together, wanting to put distance between them and the unconscious Readers before they woke.

Half way across the valley, and Jay once again sensed a movement on the ridge up to their left. She slowed but did not stop, Femi and Stitch a little way ahead of her. She covertly watched the ridge for movement, and pushed thoughts into Stitch's mind so that he'd be alert.

A definite noise this time. She stopped for a moment and craned her neck to see. A few stones scuttled down the bank just ahead of her. Stitch and Femi were way ahead and around the corner. She daren't call them. Why wasn't Stitch hearing her?

More stones, and a rock landed on the path in front of Jay. Her heart thumped. She couldn't get a handle on the power signature. Whatever it was, it was shielding.

Someone slid down the bank and landed square on the pathway in front of Jay.

'Cassie?'

'Hey!' said Cassie.

Jay bent double with the relief, feeling like she'd been winded. 'You scared the sh–'

'I've been tracking you for ages.' Cassie grinned, then pulled Jay into a hug, surprising Jay.

They lingered for a minute, and when they pulled apart, Cassie's eyes were glassy. 'You missed me?' Jay said.

Cassie grinned again. 'I found the aftermath of your fight with those Readers, so I knew I was on the right track, but I couldn't get through to you.'

'There's something about the topography here that makes it a little challenging to get communications through in certain areas.' Jay didn't understand every-thing about communication through the power. Where the energy in the environment was strong, where water flowed and vegetation thrived, communication was usually also strong. But this hadn't always been the case on Island 7. The dryness of the earth and the steep, mountainous terrain seemed to deflect their communications. 'I couldn't get through to Stitch. Look at him,' Jay motioned ahead where Stitch and Femi continued on their path, oblivious.'

Cassie laughed, and as she and Jay started walking, Stitch and Femi turned to notice them and waited up ahead. 'Are you OK?' Jay asked Cassie. 'What happened? We thought the Readers might have taken you.'

'Not likely.'

'Femi said he saw tracks. Readers had been in the cave.'

'I sat around waiting for you guys, feeling much better, when I sensed the Readers approach from above. I ducked out of the cave and as far away as I could get.'

Stitch smiled at Cassie as they came together. 'That doesn't sound like the Cassie I know,' he said, laughing. 'Can't remember the last time I saw you running away from trouble.'

Cassie shrugged. 'Yeah, well, I couldn't be sure

how much power they had, and there's something about taking these guys on alone that I don't like. The Given power multiplies with numbers. The whole is greater than the sum of the parts, like they say.'

'It's good to have you back,' said Femi. 'We're going to need all the help we can get if we're going to take out this dam.'

'Dam?' Cassie said, confused.

As they walked, Jay filled in Cassie on what had happened at the Reader camp, what she'd seen in Atta's thoughts, and their plan to get to the dam, in whatever shape they might find it.

It was obvious that Cassie was worried. They were breaking new ground. Their plan for plunging the source stone into the core was one thing, but the evolution of that plan to the protection of the stone by ensuring the unnamed river continued to flow was something else, and this was before they could even search for the stone itself.

They walked the rest of the route down into the lower parts of the valley in silence, apprehensive about the coming challenge.

Chapter 11

They stood on the ridge that jutted into the valley like a viewing platform. The spectacle before them confirmed that the images Jay had captured from Atta showed the truth. The dam rose from the surface of the river, a grey-brown construction of rock and concrete plugging the valley like a cork.

The four of them stood concealed from the view of the people working on the dam by the trees sprouting from the cliff side. At any other time, without the looming catastrophe, the view would be spectacular. On the far side of the valley, the slope was much higher – so high that the sun was hidden behind its ridge, leaving an orange glow like an aura across the high horizon.

Through the branches, the dam was complete. The

narrow section of valley chosen by the Readers was perfect for a diversion of the river. The work of the Readers looked as if it was simply finishing off – applying the final pieces. The structure of the dam was in place, and the unnamed river flowed into the parallel valley, away from the crater lake.

'It's already finished,' said Cassie.

Jay was surprised they had sensed no reduction of power in the land now that the convergence of rivers at the source had been interrupted. Stitch seemed to read her thoughts. 'You feel anything different?' he asked. Jay shook her head.

'They've only just finished by the look of it,' Femi said. 'The river valley still has water. The level looks like it is reducing, but it's there, so it's still flowing into the crater lake.'

'For now,' said Cassie. 'It won't be long before the power weakens.'

'We beat him last time,' said Stitch. 'We will beat him again. How do we deconstruct this thing?'

'What about the source stone?' Cassie asked. 'Do we know where it is?'

'No. But it's in these hills somewhere. I can feel it,' said Jay.

'Maybe further up, where those Readers were heading,' said Femi.

Jay stared at the stone and concrete construction, a

hundred feet high and just as wide at the top, reducing to a narrow plug at its base, only fifty feet wide at the level of the surface of the river. Could they destabilise it enough to free the unnamed river? 'We have to get as close as possible.'

'Can't we do it from here?' asked Stitch.

'We have only one chance and we'll be weaker from here. If the Readers clock us, they'll be crawling all over these slopes and we won't stand a chance of concentrating the power.'

'What about if I go close, you project from here and I channel your power?' Femi said.

Jay considered. 'Maybe we can combine a local power concentration at the face, like you say. Then we don't all need to get too close.'

'One of us does,' said Stitch, looking at Femi.

'I'll go,' said Jay. 'I'll be most able to shield from the Readers. I should be able to slip in and out without being detected.'

'It has to be me,' said Femi. 'I'm a pretty good shielder too, and I can climb down this cliff face better than any of you.'

Jay had mixed feelings, still not sure she could trust Femi. 'What about if we both go?' she said.

'No point,' said Stitch. 'Femi is the climber. And we need you here to channel as much power as we can from me and Cassie, and whatever you can get from Thabisa back at base.'

Femi shrugged. 'Whatever.'

Jay conceded. Yet, something didn't feel right. It seemed a little easy for them to get there. She half expected scores of Readers to emerge from the hills. 'Be careful,' she said to Femi. 'It feels dark. Atta is probably here somewhere, and if they know we're free of the camp, then they'll be on the lookout. This place will be protected.'

'There's hardly anyone here,' Cassie said, peering through the branches towards the dam. 'They must think you guys are still locked up.'

'Atta will know,' Jay said. 'If he is anywhere close, he will know.'

Femi repacked his rucksack and secured it on his back with straps around his waist. He slipped over to the edge of the platform and backed over the ledge to begin his climb. 'Hang on,' said Jay. 'Where are you planning to focus?'

Femi nodded towards the dam. 'You'll see me. The weakest plane is the front face. Everyone knows that.' He smiled. 'Where the pressure from behind pushes the structure into tension.' He motioned the pulling apart of the rock face. 'I'll find a suitable nook in that front face and get to work.'

'Signal to us when you are ready,' Jay said.

'I'll start the process from up close, then I'll signal you and back off. As soon as you see me clear the face, you get going.'

Jay nodded, keeping her eyes on the front face of the dam, imagining how the power could be channelled to set in motion the dam's destabilisation. When she looked back to Femi, he had already disappeared below the ledge.

'Tell me the logic again,' Cassie said as Jay turned back to her two best friends. She worried they were far from close to any kind of victory, and that they were once again in real danger of being overcome by the power of the darkness.

'According to Colson, the stone can't be destroyed by the Readers, or any Dark power. It can only be destroyed by Given energy.'

'Got it,' Cassie said.

'But the stone could be weakened if the flow of the unnamed river is impeded like this – by taking away the Given energy that sustains its power.'

'So then he can destroy the weakened stone?'

'Perhaps.'

Femi came into view at the foot of the dam, near the ever lowering surface of the river. The sparkle of energy remained in the water, but its power was already waning because of its reduced flow capacity.

'There he is,' said Stitch.

'Come,' Jay said, ushering Cassie and Stitch closer. They crouched, ready to connect. Jay closed her eyes and summoned help from Thabisa. Her image came quickly. She was ready. 'Now. We need your power,' Jay whispered.

With Thabisa's image came an immediate flow of Given energy that took Jay a second to control. Her ability to receive and channel Given power from remote sources was more seamless as she became more attuned. She opened her hands for Stitch and Cassie to join her. A spark of energy fizzed through each hand as Stitch and Cassie joined.

Femi side-stepped elegantly across the face of the dam and into location at its centreline. As he worked his own power, the power in Jay grew. Femi moved higher up the line of his chosen fracture plane and continued to attack the dam, before eventually moving away, back across the face of the dam to continue his work from a safe distance.

Jay opened her chest to the full flow of energy. Stitch seemed to respond with his own concentration of the power. It flowed through Jay like electricity. When Cassie too reached her peak, the three of them connected as one - like a little nuclear reactor waiting for the signal to explode.

As they watched, a crack propagated through the

dam, and water seeped through. A sparkle of light edged through the crack in the dam, as if the Given power was trying to break free from its source in the water of the unnamed river. 'Now,' Jay said, channelling the flow of Given power towards the dam.

Cassie and Stitch ratcheted up their energy flow, pouring everything they had into Jay, who amplified it with her own, and powered it towards the dam. The rocks fractured, began to delaminate and cascade into the valley below.

There were no Readers. She stood to get a better view of the dam. Cassie and Stitch moved with her so that they remained connected, and their energy continued to flow. Around them, brittle leaves on the trees fluttered, curled inwards as though singed as a palpable glow emanated from the three friends.

After a moment, the face of the dam came away, and all that was left was a glowing light. The energy focused on a small zone at the centre of their attack, where the power of the unnamed river would smash through and meander to the crater lake once more.

But the water flowed around this centre piece. The glow at the epicentre increased, a focused white light like a small sun, almost too bright to look at.

'What's happening?' Jay said, wavering.

'Nearly there,' said Stitch, gritting his teeth and

holding the line as he poured everything he had into their attack.

The explosion demolished the entire front face of the dam, and, without its key structural form to resist the high river water the other side, the rest of the dam peeled away from the edges and tumbled into the valley. The river powered through, rushing into the ravine and scattering bits of the dam along the banks.

The white light from the dam intensified, expanding to fill the sky so that the hills became invisible. Jay shielded her eyes, peeking through her fingers as the streams of energy pushed into the sky, carrying dust and debris into a small mushroom cloud.

The light faded as the mushroom cloud darkened and settled. As the darkness encroached, the bad feeling in the pit of Jay's stomach spread through her body.

'What have we done?' she said under her breath.

'Where's Femi?' called Cassie, above the noise of the gushing river.

Jay was distracted. With the explosion came a sinking sensation that dragged her to the floor. She crouched, trying to control her spinning head. What had they done? Darkness pulled at her insides until she retched. She took a breath and clamped her lips shut, then steadied her breathing. What was it that brought the darkest sense to her chest that she'd ever felt? Something was wrong. Very wrong.

She looked over at Stitch. He remained crouched on the ground, his head in his hands. He sensed Jay's gaze and looked across at her. His eyes revealed the same concern that Jay felt. 'What is it?' Stitch said. 'This feeling. What is it?'

Jay shook her head. She couldn't untangle the thoughts swishing around in her head, or suppress the growing nausea in her stomach. Why, after they'd released the power of the unnamed river, did she feel as if they had done something to have the opposite effect? The power had been depleted. Darkness was closing in.

Femi appeared back at the ledge, and Cassie reached to give him a hand up. 'Good work,' she said. Femi looked surprised at Cassie's words. 'What?' she said.

'Can't you feel it?' said Femi.

Jay dragged herself to stand. 'What is it?' she asked. 'I feel it too. What's happened?'

Femi was silent for a moment as he looked between the expectant expressions of Jay and Stitch, and the confused look on Cassie. 'The stone,' he said. 'We've destroyed the stone. It's gone.'

IN THE UNDERGROUND CAVERN, Enzo looked on as her mother reached for the cave wall to steady herself. Thabisa locked eyes with her daughter and they both knew something terrible had happened. The energy of the Given had taken a blow. Thabisa looked down at the pendant around Enzo's neck. The little stone glowed green in the darkness of the cavern.

Enzo took the stone in her hands, its green colour reflecting in her eyes. 'What's happening?' she said, tears in her eyes for all she had suffered: for her dad, her sister, and for the fall of the Given.

'I think...' Thabisa started, but couldn't complete her sentence. She took a deep breath and straightened, pushing herself away from the wall to stand unaided.

Enzo's gaze flicked from her mother to the stone and back again, her expression of sadness turning to one of fear and confusion. 'It feels weak. Look at it.' Its green shimmering light was fading.

'I think the Readers have destroyed the source stone,' Thabisa said, her voice low and shaky.

'No!' said Enzo, tears once more filling her eyes. She held the stone tight in her closed hand for a moment, as if trying to stop its power from leaking away, then allowed her fingers to relax once more. Its green shimmer faded a little, then brightened for a second before going dark, like a lightbulb in its final moments.

The stone turned a muted grey, and the cavern was dark.

Chapter 12

'It's my fault,' Jay said, burying her head in her hands again and groaning. 'He manipulated me. I let him. I think I'm going to be sick.'

'The stone was in the dam...' Stitch said.

Jay nodded. 'It was us,' she said. 'We destroyed the stone. The Readers couldn't do it, like Colson said, so they got us to do it for them.' This realisation took the strength from Jay's body and she flopped to the ground once more. Stitch went to her, put a hand on her arm.

'They led us here,' said Femi. 'Got us to do their bidding.'

'But we did it,' Cassie said. 'We destroyed the dam. The water is flowing. Look at it. The power is coming back to the crater lake.'

'Without the stone–' Jay started, but couldn't finish the sentence.

'Without the stone,' Stitch continued, 'the Reader core cannot be destroyed. We can't banish the darkness from Island 7. Atta has won.'

'No,' Cassie said, in a tone that made the word a statement of intent. 'The power is flowing again. There will be another way.'

'What other way?' Jay snapped. She pulled herself to stand, wobbly on her feet. She felt as if she'd run a marathon. She looked up into the hills. There were Readers, trekking from the remains of the dam and heading north into the peaks, under the shadow of the black dust clouds.

Femi followed her gaze. 'Where are they going?' he said.

'There's more to this,' said Jay, sensing that the Readers had more to reveal before they reached the end of this battle.

'What else can we do?' said Femi. 'Without the stone. We can never win this war.'

'Maybe not,' said Jay. 'But we can at least make sure the Given power will remain, and give those who are here a fighting chance.'

'They'll rebuild the dam,' said Femi.

Stitch joined them. 'And we'll knock it down again,' he said.

'And we'll take as many of them as we can with us as we do so,' said Cassie. 'We might not be able to destroy the connection to the core, but we can make life difficult for them at the sink facility. The concentration of their energy needs that thing to be functional. We can challenge that every day of the week if we have to.'

'Why are they heading into those hills?' Jay said, almost to herself. She would have expected them to be filing back down to their camp - mission accomplished. There was something more. 'What's up there?' she asked Femi.

'Trees, Fynbos,' Femi said.

'Something more,' Jay said under her breath.

'Let's move,' Jay said. 'We can track them. At least until we understand what's going on. Then we head back to the underground, to Thabisa, and we prepare to defend this place. We're not giving up yet.'

Chapter 13

Jay tried to hide her lack of confidence and strength. Since the explosion, the darkness weighed on her heavily, and it was all she could do to keep from collapsing. Stitch knew, of course. There was little she could hide from him. He was worried. She could tell without him needing to say anything. And, she knew that the power drain that came with the loss of the source stone had also affected Stitch. He, too, was weak.

Cassie and Femi lagged as Jay pushed on, Stitch a few feet behind her. 'Wait,' said Stitch, and Jay allowed him to catch her up. 'We need to get back. Re-group and gather our energy. If we hit Readers, we won't be any use.'

'Those two seem strong,' Jay said, motioning to Cassie and Femi.

'How come?' Stitch said. 'Why did this not affect them like I know it's affecting you and me?'

Jay shrugged. 'I guess me and you feel things deeper, eh?' She forced a half smile. Stitch linked his arm with Jay and used her to drag him along a bit. Their physical connection seemed to give Jay a little more energy. They were better as one, as had always been the case, but she sensed his trepidation. 'I just need to see,' she said. 'I have a bad feeling, and we need to know the full extent of his plans if we stand any chance of helping the Given survive in this land.'

'I know,' said Stitch. 'I have a similar bad feeling. I just have a different view of the solution. Mine takes us that way.' He nods down the hill, away from the Readers. 'And yours takes us towards trouble.'

After nearly an hour trekking into the hills, with Stitch and Femi taking a lead in tracking the Readers, Jay's energy was at its lower limits. Cassie helped her along. 'We need to get you back down,' Cassie said, a look of concern.

'As soon as we figure this out.'

Femi and Stitch came to a halt up ahead. 'What is it?' asked Cassie as they reached them.

Femi raised a hand for Cassie to be quiet. He nodded towards a ridge over the valley up ahead. 'Readers,' he said.

Jay strained to see. 'Just two of them?' she said.

'I think one of them is injured,' said Stitch.

Jay tapped into her power to see if she could confirm Stitch's suspicion, but felt nothing. 'Are they alone?' she asked.

'Wait here,' said Femi, and moved as if to head into the trees between them and the Readers.

'Where are you going?' asked Cassie.

'See if our friends have anything to say about what the hell has just happened?'

'Wait,' said Cassie. 'I'm coming.'

Jay too staggered forwards but Cassie turned and told her to stay. 'You'll be no help in your state. Wait here. Take a moment to recover. We'll see what we can find out.' She turned to Stitch. 'Look after her.' Stitch nodded, and Cassie disappeared into the trees behind Femi.

Jay and Stitch slumped to the floor in a position from which they had a good view over to the Readers. They were out in the open just in front of the tree line, perfectly positioned for Femi and Cassie to approach unseen. 'You think they'll be OK?' asked Stitch.

'They're stronger than those two Readers,' Jay put a hand on Stitch's hand. She needed to feel his energy and his warmth. She was close to the end of her rope. The darkness in her belly weighed heavily. He turned his hand so that he could thread his fingers between Jay's, and he squeezed tight. 'What are we doing here,

Stitch?' Jay said, casting her eyes around them and looking up into the trees. 'It's all happened so fast,' she said. 'It doesn't feel like long ago we were having a sleepover round my place with mountains of crisps and sweets. And now we're on the side of a hill somewhere in South Africa.'

Stitch laughed. 'Give me the mountain of sweets any day.'

'I'll take the monster munch,' Jay said.

They were quiet a moment, then Stitch said, 'There was always going to be something more for you. We knew that. Even when we were kids, I knew you'd be special. You were special, even back then.'

'You always had faith in me. Even when I was screwing everything up.' Jay stole a glance at her friend, her best friend for as long as she could remember, and one of the most reliable constants in her life. She followed the lines in his face from the corners of his eyes as he squinted into the sun. He'd aged rapidly over the past year, like they all had. And his facial features were strengthening. She tried to think if he looked anything like his dad, and decided that apart from his skin tone - a pale brown - there was little resemblance. 'You look more and more like your mum, you know?'

'Really?'

Jay nodded. 'That photo you have in your hallway

downstairs, with your mum when she was young. You look like her.'

Stitch smiled. 'Mum's looks and Dad's brains - best of both.'

'You tell yourself that, my friend.' She squeezed his hand, just as Femi and Cassie burst from the foliage down on the ledge, startling the two Readers. Only one of the Readers stood, the other remaining on the ground as if too hurt to move. Cassie and Femi were clearly too much for him as they fought. He fell, stumbling and rolling perilously close to the edge of the ridge, below which was nothing but hundreds of feet of drop onto rocks.

He scrambled back from the edge, Femi standing over him. Cassie turned her attention to the other Reader, kicking out at him when he attempted to stand. 'Shall we go over there?' said Stitch.

Jay nodded, and Stitch helped her stand. They pushed through the bushes and into the trees. The shouts from the ridge below became louder, and Jay sensed the Readers weren't giving up without a fight.

Dark power flowed, and a piercing scream shattered the stillness. It didn't sound like Cassie.

'Let's move,' she said.

They picked up speed, slashing their way towards the sounds of the fighting and at last emerged onto the rocks just down from the ledge.

'There,' said Stitch, pointing over to where Femi stood over the prone body of one of the Readers, as Cassie peered over the edge. No sign of the other Reader. Stitch glanced at Jay before climbing down to join the others.

'Where's the other one?' Stitch said.

Cassie motioned over the ledge, then lowered her gaze as if she was ashamed.

'What happened?' asked Jay.

'He did it to himself,' Cassie said, looking over to Femi for support. 'He threw himself off.'

Femi nodded without taking his eyes off the other Reader.

'Why?' Stitch said. The fear on the face of the other Reader gave a hint to why. He feared what they might do, for sure, especially Femi, who was keeping the Reader close to the ledge. But he feared what Atta might do to him if he were to betray the cause of the Dark.

'He knows something,' said Jay.

Femi nodded again, taking his eyes off the Reader for a moment to acknowledge Jay. 'It's coming,' Femi said, and Jay realised Femi wasn't threatening the Reader with being thrown off the ledge. He was stopping him from following his mate to the bottom of the gorge.

Jay crouched down, her legs still wobbly, and her energy levels low. The Dark was everywhere.

'Help me out here, Cassie,' said Femi, keeping a hold on the Reader. 'There's something coming through but I need a bit of help.'

Cassie joined Femi, and Stitch too stood over the Reader. The Reader's resolve weakened. His thoughts seeped from him as Femi squeezed, using his characteristic combination of Given and Dark power.

'No,' the Reader grunted, his eyes fixed on Femi, and his expression one of surprise at Femi's ability to break him, and fear at the information he was leaking. 'No,' he croaked, and squeezed his eyes tight in concentration.

His thoughts and knowledge flowed like the flow of the unnamed river through the dam.

In the hills was the origin of the unnamed river.

Jay frowned inwardly. So what? A river's true source can be scattered widely, with many elements flowing in from a catchment.

This source was more powerful. This was something else. It was the magical origin. The source of the energy that flows to create the power of the unnamed river – the Origin.

Femi opened his eyes and exchanged a glance with Jay. She nodded for him to continue.

The Reader was broken. His mind lay open like a book. He mumbled and rambled indecipherable words.

Jay read him. There was a way to destroy the magic that created the origin of power to the unnamed river. Whilst there were a multitude of sources of the river itself, there was only a single source of its power, the Origin. And this power could be destroyed.

'How?' Jay said aloud. The answers came with no resistance, and the reason that the Readers had kept the body of Tiago became clear.

The means to extinguish the Origin of Given power to the unnamed river, was something to do with the death of Tiago and his connected C, Annika. Tiago and Annika were essentially created by the energy of the Origin, and the power of the Given, and it was their deaths, their remains, that could end that same power.

The readers had been trawling the hills for months if not years, hunting for the origin of Given power that flowed into the unnamed river. Not just on Island 7, but on all the Islands. They had Readers dedicated to finding these sparks of energy, so that Atta's ultimate plan to extinguish the Given power on all the islands could be realised. There was no way of knowing how close Atta had come to finding the Origin on their own Island 8 – perhaps Jay's successful destruction of the connection to the core had come just in time, before the darkness overcame and purged the Given energy from her homeland.

On Island 7, they had located this spark, and with the death of Tiago and Annika, the Readers had what they needed to destroy the source of Given power.

Once again, Femi turned to Jay, his expression now grave. As he did so, the Reader broke free from his grasp and rolled himself over the edge without a sound.

Femi turned to reach for him but it was too late.

Chapter 14

The power of the unnamed river drew Jay close. She needed to recharge, and, feeling that power, knowing that the source of Given power on Island 7 remained, reassured her. There was time to rest.

Stitch and Femi built a fire from wood gathered nearby. The roof of the cave near the entrance sloped up and out into the valley, so with the fire near the opening, the buoyant smoke rose and followed the slope of the ceiling out into the open air.

Jay patrolled the entrance to the cave, smoke rising above her head. Further along the valley, the remains of the dam continued to be washed away by the relentless flow of the river, forcing its way down towards Kaapstown and the coast. It must have taken the Readers months to build the dam, and then to embed the source stone within it, in a location they knew would be the focus of energy of any attack by Given power. Atta had once again manipulated her and her friends into getting what he needed. And this time, she could see no easy way out.

'Strangely beautiful,' said Stitch.

'Thanks,' Jay said with a wry smile.

'Not you... I mean, you are, of course, but I meant...'

Jay laughed. 'I'm kidding, you idiot. The river. These hills.' She took a deep breath of the cool, fresh air flowing through the valley with the water. 'It's good to know they haven't killed everything yet.'

Stitch nodded, reading Jay's emotions. She couldn't stand the thought of the Readers reducing this environment to one without the river; without trees; and without the foliage spread through the valley, which would surely wither and eventually die if the Readers took full control.

'The odds are stacking up,' Jay said.

Cassie joined them. 'Exactly when we perform best,' she said, with her characteristic optimism and hunger for a battle. A crack of burning wood sent sparks into the roof of the cave. Femi fed in another log then headed out to join the others.

'So,' said Femi. 'This was all a diversion.' He nodded towards the remains of the dam.

'All part of his grand plan,' said Jay. 'Suckered us in.'

'At least we know what their plan is now,' said Cassie. 'We just need to work on ours.'

Femi made to say something but stopped himself. Jay told him to speak his mind. 'It's just something I saw in that Reader. You saw it too, I think?' Femi said.

She had. Before he rolled himself over the edge, he'd recognised Jay and Stitch, or at least recognised their power signature, and took solace in their presence. She had pushed it around inside her head, but couldn't make sense of it. 'What did you make of it?' she asked.

'We know now that the Island 8C and his connected C threaten the source, right?'

Jay nodded. Stitch said, 'Yes.'

'That Reader. He was thinking that it doesn't have to be the 8C and the C from this Island. It could be those from another Island.'

They were silent for a moment. This aligned with what Jay had felt from the Reader. 'So me and Stitch could be used to destroy the Origin of the source on this Island as well as our own?'

'Or any Island,' said Femi.

'But they don't need me and Jay here,' said Stitch. 'They already have what they need.'

'As far as we know,' said Femi. 'The reality is that

171

we don't know that they haven't drawn us here to use Jay and Stitch.'

'Not likely,' said Cassie. 'We have to assume they have what they need, and we have to make sure they don't get to the Origin with the remains of Tiago and Annika.'

'If you're right,' Jay said, interrupting Cassie and turning to Femi, 'then me and Stitch could be a liability.'

'Exactly,' said Femi.

'But we need you if we are to get anywhere near overpowering the Readers,' said Cassie.

After a minute, Jay said, 'What choice do we have?' No one answered. 'We have to risk it.' Jay made her way back towards the fire, feeling the chill now that the last of the sun had slipped behind the hills to the west. 'We can't afford to let this divert us,' she said.

Femi called after her, 'We can't afford to ignore it. If we stop them using Tiago and Annika, then what's their next move? It's you.'

'Then we won't let it come to that,' said Jay, her tone ending the discussion.

Her energy levels remained low, and she had no motivation to argue. The pathway was clear. The only thing to do was protect the Origin. She slumped onto the floor by the fire, her head lolling, and her vision fading fast.

'Hey,' Stitch rushed over to her. 'Rest back.' He guided Jay to rest against the rocks, holding his hand to her forehead to check for a fever.

'Is she hot?' asked Femi.

Stitch shook his head. 'Cold, if anything.'

'I'm OK,' Jay said, slurring her words. She shivered uncontrollably.

'Losing the source stone took something of Jay with it. We need to rest here and get her strong before we can even think about Readers.'

'Can't you heal?' Cassie said.

Jay sensed Stitch come closer, his hand on her arm. His warmth flowed through her body and it was comforting. She stopped shivering and her body weighed heavily on the floor of the cave. Fatigue washed over her in waves and she slipped further down into a more horizontal position.

'I can't do it. I don't really know what's wrong with her so the healing has no focus, nothing to target.'

'Try again,' said Cassie.

Stitch kept his hand on Jay and the warm glow continued, slowly ejecting the shreds of coldness stabbing at her insides. She leaned into him, grateful. 'I'll be OK, Stitch,' she said. 'Just stay with me for a while.'

He moved nearer, wrapping his arms and warmth around her until, comforted by his warmth and strength, she drifted into a deep sleep.

When she woke, the other three were all asleep, and the fire had died to glowing embers. She had a blanket over her and a sleeping bag under her head for a pillow. Her mind was alert, but her body still felt weak.

She sat up and placed two logs onto the fire from a pile by the rocks. Smoke rose as the heat quickly penetrated to the core of the wood, burning off the moisture. She hugged her knees.

Stitch snored. She'd recognise that noise anywhere. Femi and Cassie were quiet, their sleeping bags rising and falling in rhythm.

The sky beyond the opening to the cave was black, its only visible feature a single star high above the hills opposite. The moon, if it was out there somewhere, was probably concealed in the clouds. She leaned her head back against the wall of the cave and took a deep breath, enjoying the silence.

The power inside Jay sent mixed messages. Why could it not be clear, like it was back home? The environment of Island 7 seemed to confuse her signals. The energy of the Given – a normally distinct and powerful source of energy, was stifled here, was less profound than the Given power in her own homeland. There were reasons for this. She knew that. Tiago was dead. His connected C also dead. And now the source stone's destruction has left a gaping hole in the power.

Then there was the Dark. Was there a role for the Dark power in the hands of the Given?

Femi had badgered Jay from the beginning to be open to the potential of the darkness as a supplement to the power of the Given. She was not so sure. She had felt its tainting of the pure potential of Given power, and she had seen firsthand the consequences of opening to the power of the darkness. Opening a channel to the controller of the Dark, Atta, would be asking for trouble, and allowing him access to her – and to those she loves.

Stitch too aligned with Femi's thinking. He pushed her not to dismiss the potential. She searched her intuition. They would need something extra if they were to salvage something of a future for Island 7. The Event, back in her homeland, had created something of a fusing of Given and Dark energy within her, and despite her best efforts to expel the darkness, she knew deep down that it remained. It was dormant, but it was there.

Sloping back onto her side, Jay pulled in her knees to assume the foetal position. To the sound of the crackling of the fire, she closed her eyes and allowed the wisps of energy within her take their own paths as she drifted back into sleep.

Chapter 15

The next morning, above the dawn chorus, the noise from the river was angrier than the night before.

Jay lay watching her friends for signs of wakefulness. Stitch was so quiet she had to stare for a while to make sure he was breathing. His sleeping bag rose and fell in a shallow rhythm. She smiled into the gloom, thinking that it had been a long time since she'd seen Stitch asleep without the accompaniment of his snoring.

Wide awake, she crawled out from under her blanket and stretched, then made for the entrance to the cave. Down in the valley, the river roared, cutting through the rocks. She looked up into the distance, where the hills steepened and dissolved into the mist and clouds. She wondered how so much water could be channelled into a single flow of such power. At its origin, they would find the spark of energy.

Little remained of the dam, but the rock fill in the side sections out of reach of the water's flow. As Jay gazed at the sparkling flow of water, something caught her eye. A green light fizzed across the surface once more and Jay's breathing faltered. She strained to see it again. She stood and looked back at the sleeping forms of her friends before stepping quietly from the cave.

The pathway soon fizzled out as the undergrowth thickened near the banks of the river. It was as if the trees and bushes conspired to conceal the river, to protect it. It reminded her of how the unnamed river back on Island 8, her homeland, was almost impossible to get to if you didn't know its precise location. The difference here was that the river was over ten times wider, carrying vastly more flow. Its physical power was immense. If they could protect the magical source, the Origin, then there was surely a chance for this river to bring enough power to the Given to enable the protection of this land.

She emerged through the trees to the rocky banks of the river. The sky had lightened from its dark grey to a murky, cloudless colour. At close range, the noise of the river was deafening. A light spray carried on the wind buffeted Jay, cooling her face. The surface of the water surged and swelled as it hurried downstream, swirling as it went, circling to look back at Jay as it turned the corner in the distance. She wiped the moisture from her cheeks and moved to head upstream to the remains of the dam.

Up close, the sheer scale of the dam was staggering. It had been built with a thick base, rising some two or three hundred feet to a narrow top. Through its demolished structure, Jay could see its makeup of rocks – from bigger boulders at its base with infill stones packed in, to smaller rocks. The front face of the dam had been finished with a kind of mud that had dried like concrete. She ran her hand over the rough surface of a section of dam that had escaped the destruction. She wondered if they'd built this entire construction, which must have taken months, purely to conceal the stone. Atta had patience for sure. He was far from impulsive. He would bide his time, putting all the required elements of his plan together without urgency. If there was anyone who could play the long game with a sacrificial dam, then perhaps it was Atta.

The river rushed at its fastest through the area of the demolished dam, where it narrowed slightly from the main section. The surface bubbled and frothed over the demolished rocks.

And then Jay saw it again. A sparkle of light.

Just the movement of water? A reflection of sunlight?

Light shimmered once more and Jay moved closer, stepping out over the water to an island of rocks poking above the water. She edged her way across the stones, closer to the middle, where the light shimmered.

A rock from the remains of the dam tumbled into the water from the side of the cliff. The river swallowed it without a sound.

Jay teetered on her rock for a moment, disorientated by the noise, the swirling wind and the fine spray that dampened her skin. She gathered herself and rubbed water from her face before stepping further into the river from rock to rock.

Almost at the centre, she crouched closer to the surface of the water and pulled up her hood to protect herself from the cold, wet wind. She saw no light. No shimmer emanating from the deep. No sparkle of power from a surviving source stone.

Nothing.

The river water swelled and danced around her, white froth spitting as it travelled downstream. She stood and breathed in the cool air, resisting the urge to scream into the wind.

As she stepped back over the rocks towards the bank, a section of the foot of the dam gave way. Rocks from above scuttled down the slope – small stones and gravel at first, but then larger sections as the structure was undermined.

Rocks continued to fall. Jay realised she was in real danger. Her heart pounded as she searched for a safe route back to the riverbank. The falling rocks gathered momentum, bigger and bigger pieces cascading into the water between her and the bank.

There was another possible route, if she could stretch to jump between rocks further apart. Even if she went into the water, she might be OK.

She took a breath and jumped to the first set of rocks, her foot slipping into the water. She crunched her shin and screamed out, but managed to pull herself up onto the flat surface. The next stepping stone was further away, and smaller. Her leg throbbed with pain, and she could only tentatively rest her weight on it as the pain shot through her leg to her knee.

More rocks slid down the cliff edge, gathering pace like an avalanche. The entire area was unstable. The entire side of the valley was ready to slide into the water and take Jay with it. As the thought spun through her mind, the hill above her moved as if fulfilling her prophecy.

Chapter 16

Her heart stopped, and the noise was swallowed up as time slowed. She focused her energy into the time freeze. Even on Island 8, her ability to freeze or slow time was unreliable. She opened her chest to the power, and time slowed further. Something caught her eye.

Femi stood on the rocky bank.

Time stopped for everything except her and Femi.

He held out his hand for Jay to reach. Rocks above their heads slowed to a stop in mid air, threatening to engulf them both in tonnes of debris.

Jay reached out for Femi's hand and threw herself towards him.

He pulled her onto the bank, and they scrambled downstream, away from the dam as time wound itself back into motion once more. A deafening crash like thunder from behind them. Jay turned to see a wedge of the hill slide into the water and immediately become swept away downstream. Femi ushered Jay to a log, a fallen tree near the edge of the river. 'Rest a moment,' he said.

Jay's thoughts twisted around what had just happened – how she had stopped time like she used to back home. She turned to Femi. 'It was you... How?'

Femi took a seat beside Jay and let out a sigh. 'Not just me. Both of us combined. I've only done that once before, and it was nothing as impressive as that.' He gave Jay an uncharacteristic grin. 'It must have been the combination of our power.'

'I don't know,' Jay said, confused at what Femi had achieved. He was a level seven. No level seven could affect time like that. Even level eights had no time control. Only her, and her old enemy, Marcus, to some degree, when he was raging. 'I've not got enough power to do that here on Island 7.'

'If you dig deep, and make the best of the energy here, I think you'll find you can achieve a lot more than you think.'

Jay turned away from Femi and looked back up into the hills towards the cave.

'They're still asleep. I sensed something and then

noticed you were gone so I tracked you down here. I can feel your emotions clearly, you know that?'

Jay gave a reluctant nod. Femi's talent for connecting to her unnerved her.

'Any sign of anything in there?' Femi nodded towards the water by the dam.

'There's power there. The Origin must still be alive, at least for now. I was hoping for something of the source stone to be there, but nothing I could find before the cliff tried to swallow me whole.'

'Clutching at straws,' said Femi.

Jay felt a wave of dizziness and rested her elbows on her knees, her head in her hands. Femi seemed to read her weakness but said nothing, instead placing a hand on her shoulder that passed some of his own energy to her. He seemed to transmit power as easily as Stitch.

'Thanks,' she said.

Femi was quiet for a moment, then said, 'Can I tell you something?'

'I guess.'

'About my father.' He lowered his head.

'What happened to him?'

'Killed by the first Readers to arrive here.'

Jay turned to look Femi in the eye. 'I'm sorry. Did he have power?'

Femi shook his head. 'Tiago and Thabisa were off

on a mission with my mother when the Readers came to the house.'

'What happened?'

'They came for my mother I think, as the Island's connected C. It was before the Readers had any significant power in this land, before the emergence of Atta, and way before we retreated underground, when the City was lost to the darkness.

'Who were they?'

'We think they were forward scouts from their previous Island conquest. From Island six or five. Three of them entered our house. They were each powerful as individuals, but together, they were invincible. I was surprised. We had not encountered Readers with such power before. I remember their elder, with his long robes, jewellery, and he had the most prominent of scars on the side of his head, here.' He motioned to his temple. 'I will never forget that face. One day, I will avenge my father's death. And that of my mother.'

'How long ago was your father killed?'

'Six years,' Femi said without hesitation. 'But it is still fresh in my head.'

'He is clever.'

'Atta?'

Jay nodded. 'Even before he has a significant hold

on an Island, he reaches in with his evil tentacles and prepares the ground for damage.'

'The Given should have seen it coming,' Femi said. 'They failed to prepare, and my father paid the price. I had to watch him die – shrivel into the dust. He was no match for the power of the Readers.'

'I'm sorry.' Jay's gaze lingered on Femi for a moment. She read him. She saw that his anger at the Given's inability to protect his family tempted him to explore the darkness.

He returned her gaze, as if aware of being read. 'Yes. I explore it. That doesn't make me one of them. It makes me more of an asset to the Given. Harder to break down by Readers.'

'But this is not the way,' said Jay.

'Why not?' Femi snapped. 'It's not simply a case of good against evil. It's about the use of the power, what you do with it, not where it comes from.'

'It's poisonous.'

'That's in your head. Pure emotion. Use your brain. Think about it. Open to it.'

Jay huffed and avoided Femi's gaze once more. She looked to the environment around her for support but received nothing.

She thought of a discussion she'd had with Stitch about the darkness before she'd cut the conversation short, refusing to debate it. Stitch talked about the super-position of the powers. He talked about the power being like a waveform rising and falling with defined peaks and troughs. He said that the powers are of the same frequency, and without moderation, the combination of Dark and Given power can have a cancelling effect, like a sound wave cancelled by an inverse wave as in noise cancelling. Stitch had a way of relating non-physical phenomena to a base in science, in physics. He said that if you can control the two waveforms, Dark and Given, then you can moderate so that their peaks coincide, as well as their troughs, so that they synchronise, superimposing their power and creating a doubly intense energy. What if Stitch was right? What if Femi was already putting into practise the physics that Stitch felt was true?

'I'm scared,' Jay admitted, surprising herself at her candidness.

'Me too,' said Femi, his tone softer. 'I need your help. And I can help you. Come.' He stood. 'Let me show you something.

Femi led Jay into the trees at the edge of the river, and then down a shallow slope to where he stopped at the foot of a cliff. 'Here,' he said, crouching by a hole in the floor; a crevice in the rocks that seemed to stretch deep into the ground. Jay was surprised to see that it was dry, being below the level of the adjacent river.

'Do you feel the warmth?'

Jay leaned down and felt warm air rising through the crevice in the rock. She rocked back on her heels at the darkness of the power.

'These channels of power are everywhere here, on Island seven. Whatever happens up there,' he motioned into the hills, 'we cannot defend ourselves in the longer term on this Island without connecting to the deeper sources of power, be they Dark or Given. We are overpowered.'

Jay waited. Femi had more to say. He crouched by the hole in the floor and allowed the energy of the darkness to flow over him, through him. Jay sensed the combining of the power within him. He had done this before. It was seamless. She stepped back as his power grew and pushed her away. Its strength was undeniable – greater than that expected of a level seven. He stood, but remained focused on the power source from below, coaxing it, toying with it, and bringing it under his control. Femi's streams of Given power, the white-green light, became interweaved with dark strands that tightened and strengthened the wisps of white and piercing green, sewing them together like a rope of pure power.

Femi turned to Jay, his eyes now open and the energy within him bubbling over. She sensed aggression from him and immediately put up her defences, shielding herself from his power. Femi pushed out at

Jay, forcing her arms by her side so that she couldn't lift them when she tried. She struggled to step away from him; he stopped her. Rooted to the floor, her breathing became laboured as his power brought a crushing weight to her chest. He stepped closer, his eyes faraway and his energy bringing pain.

'Stop it!' she screamed. Jay scrambled away from him, her back up against the cliff face. He raised his hands to reassure her he meant no harm. 'Stay back,' Jay said, but she was no longer scared. She was mad. Her anger grew and as Femi continued towards her, she drew on the power of the Given and pushed out at Femi, landing him on his back on the floor. He groaned, the wind taken from him.

'I'm sorry,' he said. 'I had to show you. It's powerful.'

'Not so powerful lying on your back gasping for air, are you?' Jay said, pacing.

Femi stood and before he could speak, Jay shouted, 'What was it? What did you do? How did you immobilise me like that?'

Femi remained calm. 'I think you know.'

'The Dark?'

Femi sighed, as if annoyed to have to explain himself. 'Integration,' he said. 'Like you, I have a connection with the Dark. Mine has come from hours, days, weeks or nurturing my abilities. Yours came to you with no such effort – handed on a plate.'

Jay snorted. 'I don't think what we went through at the sink room on eight was what I'd call handed on a plate. We fought with everything we had.'

'And now you reject what you have? You reject the power with which you've been entrusted? You are a level 8 Given, from Island 8. You are perhaps the last level 8, yet you reject the opportunity to save this island. What is wrong with you?' He turned away.

'I don't reject it,' Jay snapped. Then, calmer, she said, 'But I've relied before on those who use the darkness and purport to be friends of the Given.' Jay thought about Flick and the events that led to Alf's death.

'I know,' said Femi, a pleading tone to his voice. 'I'm not asking you to relinquish control to the Dark. I'm simply asking you to open to the possibility of manipulating it to supplement your own Given power. You are in control. Like Stitch says–'

'You talked to Stitch about this?' Jay said, interrupting Femi.

Femi nodded and released a heavy sigh. Jay crouched on the floor, resting her head in her hands. The hole into the earth was just a few feet away. She felt its power flowing like oil from a well. She looked at Femi, resting back against the rocks on the other side of the little clearing they'd found themselves in. He looked defeated.

As the dark power flowed, Jay turned to it. She breathed it in and reached deeper inside of herself.

JAY OPENED TO THE DARKNESS, and as it flowed through her, it felt wrong. It always felt wrong. The proximity and strength of the Dark flowing up through the ground penetrated deep within Jay, awakening the dormant power that had been a part of her ever since the Event. This new energy twisted together as one with her innate Given power.

Jay's colours emerged from her body – her natural yellows and greens with the dark grey and black of the darkness entwining and twisting around the Given colours. She resisted, instinctively. The darkness withdrew like a snake exposed to a flame. Signals from Femi told Jay to relax, to allow the darkness to come. She took a deep breath and allowed it to flow once more. It twisted and tangled around the streams of her Given energy. Then it tightened, as if trying to strangle the Given power from her.

'Don't fight it,' Femi said, standing over Jay.

His own colours emerged from his body in a way Jay had not seen before. They were unhindered, set free and pouring from him in streams of orange and red. He coached Jay through the integration of the power. 'Lose your preconceptions. Don't think about it as darkness. Feel it for the power that it is. It's not the darkness that is evil, it is how the power is interpreted and then implemented. The power is as pure as the Given energy.'

Jay opened herself further, allowing it to feel its way around her own energy. She tried to do as Femi said. She imagined the dark streams of energy integrating with her own power, joining with it and strengthening it like reinforcement in strands of vine, or steel bars set into concrete foundations. The process was as much one of the control of her mind as it was the opening of her chest to the power. If her concentration drifted for a moment, the darkness turned, tightened, and brought a bitter taste to her mouth. With focus, the darkness supported her Given energy, empowered her.

Femi reached out a hand for Jay to pull her up, but Jay couldn't move her limbs. She stared at his hand, unable to take it. Femi repeated words of encouragement like a mantra, as if he needed to pound his truth into Jay until she too believed it. 'It's not bad or evil,' he said. 'It provides a diversity and resilience to your power. It's like a second string to your bow, another army to take into battle.'

Jay breathed into the energy, allowing it to integrate more fully with her own innate power. She looked at Femi as his colours emerged with great force, twisting around his body like a tornado. He had opened himself up, hiding nothing. His positive orange and yellows mixed and glowed red with his determination. He kept his hand outstretched and seemed to draw Jay's colours from her body - her own yellows and greens seeping into the air and mixing with Femi's colours. Femi held tight to Jay's power, controlling the rate at which her energy flowed. His hand outstretched, he drew out her darkness little by little, so that it was revealed, out in the open and mixing with their colours.

Jay stood, feeling in full the strength of the combined power, and understanding how it could be controlled and used for good. She stepped closer to Femi so that their twisting, streaming colours became one. They merged. Femi pushed his energy out through his body and around Jay. She stepped back with the force of it, and her darkness twisted around her head, flowing up into the branches above.

Jay looked. The dark energy charred the leaves above her head.

Her heart pounded. She could cause damage to her environment by her reckless use of darkness. As the leaves shrivelled, she looked at Femi.

Femi pushed his own energy through to Jay once more, his expression determined. His own darkness surrounded Jay and pulled her in. 'Focus,' he said. 'Interpret this power as you need it. Let it damage only what you want damaged.' Jay looked up at the dark streams of her energy and tightened her fists, pulling the darkness back into her clouds of colours where it combined once more. The leaves in the branches above immediately recovered, and Jay's confidence grew. She allowed her power to flow more strongly, and the branches above her seemed to respond by leaning in towards her. Her energy flowed then, like a powerful river.

The energy from below her feet flowed up through her body, a mix of Given and Dark. She closed her eyes.

The vines and branches around her drew in with the force of the power. They twisted around her body as Femi stepped back and watched. Roots from below the ground broke free and tangled around her feet and legs.

Like she'd only felt occasionally, and never on Island 7, Jay felt as one with the environment, where the lines between her own physical body and nature became indistinct.

She gasped, euphoric.

She opened her eyes to see the sparkle of power surrounding her. Femi smiled.

The vines gradually retreated, and Jay and Femi's colours eventually thinned as if washed away by the wind.

Femi raised his eyebrows, and Jay nodded. 'I get it,' she said. 'I understand, now.'

Chapter 17

When Femi and Jay arrived back at the cave, Cassie stormed over to Jay. 'Where were you? You can't just wander off saying nothing.'

'Told you she was OK,' Stitch said to Cassie.

Jay motioned to Stitch. 'I got a message to Stitch. I said we were fine. Did he not tell you?'

'Yeah, but you know what he's like...'

'Charming,' said Stitch.

'As far as communication goes between me and Stitch, it's pretty reliable,' said Jay.

'Yeah, well, it would be good if you just let me know next time.'

Jay apologised to Cassie and turned to Stitch, trying to interpret the grin on his face. 'What is it?'

'Nothing,' Stitch said. 'Just trying not to say I told you so.'

Jay knew that Stitch probably deserved to enjoy the moment that vindicated his view that Jay needed to work with her inner darkness, not against it. He had clearly sensed what had happened to Jay down by the river. 'So it turns out there's something in what you were saying.'

'You drew it out? The darkness?'

Jay motioned to Femi. 'He dragged it out of me.'

Femi gave a guarded smile. 'I started the process. It is up to you to control it. Just remember that it is you who determines the focus of the combined power. If you allow it to channel itself, it will remain a power for the Dark, but if you apply your own direction, then it is like we saw down by the river.'

'I will have to be careful,' Jay said. 'I'm not really sure if I'm there yet.'

'Why did you reject its influence before now? After the Event?' Femi asked.

'I didn't trust it.'

'Or perhaps you didn't trust yourself?'

Jay shrugged. 'Who knows. I don't feel like talking about it anymore.'

Cassie looked at Femi with distrust. 'Just keep your darkness away from me, and keep him away from me,' she said, nodding at Femi.

'Let's just all drop it now,' Jay said. 'I need to concentrate.' She'd felt a wave of influence from the Readers and staggered on her feet. She looked at Femi, then to Stitch for confirmation of her senses. 'What?' said Stitch.

'You feel that?'

'No,' said Stitch. Femi, too, shook his head.

Stitch held on to Jay's arm as a second wave came, nearly knocking her off her feet. 'I got something that time,' he said. 'What is it?'

'They've found it,' said Jay. Through the power, she sensed the Readers had located the source of the magic of the unnamed river, or at least the vicinity.

'The Origin?' said Cassie.

Femi stepped back from the group and slumped down on a rock, an uncharacteristic fear etched on his face. 'They've been searching for months, years maybe. As long as I can remember, there have been Readers, scouts, in the hills. There have always been sightings – Readers from one of the Islands, on a reconnaissance mission, hunting for something in the hills.'

'You knew?' said Cassie. 'That they were looking for the Origin?'

'No,' said Femi. 'It was just stories. Like the bogey man. Shadows and ghosts in the hills. No one ever knew the truth of their presence, let alone what they might have been looking for.'

'And now it looks like they've found it,' said Stitch.

Jay nodded. 'We need to go. Before they destroy it.'

'How do we know they've not already destroyed it?' asked Cassie.

Stitch and Jay both shook their heads at the same time. Jay sensed that Stitch also knew from his senses that the Origin remained active for now. 'If what we saw in that Reader was true, they will need the remains of Tiago and Annika.'

'They are back at the camp,' said Stitch.

'Let's go,' said Femi, picking up his rucksack. 'We need to get to the Origin before it's too late.'

'But what if it's a trap? What if they need Jay and me? What if we are the ones who can facilitate the destruction of the Origin?'

Cassie paced. 'I thought it was Tiago and Annika?'

'It is,' said Jay. 'But me and Stitch could be substitutes to achieve the same effect. We don't know. That's just a chance. Anyway, what choice do we have? They already have what they need...'

'So we think,' said Cassie.

'We take that chance, or, either way, the Origin is destroyed.'

'If we are going,' said Femi. 'We need to be quick. If the Origin is destroyed, the Given power here will die, and we will be vulnerable.'

'What's the plan?' said Cassie.

Jay looked at the floor. 'We need to split up. Some of us will head to the Origin. We can't afford to allow the Readers to dominate. We need to protect it, and for this, we will have to fight. But there's a chance they haven't yet moved the remains of Tiago and Annika. We also need to head back to the camp and make sure those remains get nowhere near the Origin.'

'You three head up,' said Cassie. 'I'll go back to the camp for the remains.'

'We can split into two groups,' said Jay.

'No,' said Cassie. 'You need as many as you can up at the Origin. I will stay under the radar. In and out.'

'You sure?' Jay placed a hand on Cassie's arm. She felt Cassie's determination.

'What are we waiting for?' said Femi, edging towards the entrance to the cave.

'I need to connect with Angie. We will need her help in navigating with the Dark energy. She has a vision that we can use.'

Jay crouched on the floor of the cave and closed her eyes. Stitch and Cassie both went to her, each placing a hand on her shoulder. She felt their energy. Stitch's power came strong, a twitch of darkness in his energy that teased with Jay's own newfound power signature.

Angie came rushing at Jay as if she'd been waiting for her to connect. 'Jay,' she said, an urgency in her voice.

Her image came into focus in Jay's mind. 'We need you, Angie,' she said.

'We're here. Me and Colson. I have been feeling your power breaking out from Island 7. Are you OK?'

Jay explained the theory of the Origin. Angie seemed unsurprised, like she and Colson had already talked about it. 'We sensed it,' Angie said. 'Colson says it is probably true. And, if they find it, destroy it, then all will be lost.'

'Can you help us?' said Jay. 'We've been working with the dark energy as a supplement to the Given power. But we need your help. You too have some ability with the darkness. Can you help guide us through to the Origin? There will be resistance like we've not seen before.'

Angie was quiet for a minute. She conversed with Colson in hushed tones that Jay couldn't hear. When she came back, she was bubbly and excited. 'We can connect like we did before. Colson thinks that your connection with the darkness, and Femi too, will help us. We might be able to shield you as you head in… hang on.' Angie trailed off as she went back to Colson. 'He says that this is all new and we don't know what will happen. He worries a lot.'

Jay smiled at Angie's mocking of Colson. Those two were becoming close through their work with the literature on the history of the powers. Colson adored poring over the papers, the old books, deciphering hidden meaning. Angie liked the practical – the connection with her power, communicating with Jay, and using her gift to explore and control the darkness as well as the Given power. 'What's he worried about?'

'He says there is a risk with the combination of the Dark and Given power, that an Event could occur, like happened here.'

'But we're nowhere near the core,' said Jay.

'We just don't know. Colson says that it is the combination of Dark and Given that creates the energy imbalance that caused the Event. This is different, but there is still an energy conflict.'

'Cassie is heading back to the camp to see if she can retrieve the remains of Tiago and Annika,' said Jay.

There was a brief silence, then Angie said, 'Colson says that's a good idea. If you are right about the Origin, then if we keep the remains and the Origin separate, then it cannot be destroyed.'

'We will need you,' repeated Jay.

'We're here,' said Angie, her image fading.

Cassie and Stitch let their hands drift away from Jay and the three of them stood in silence. They had each heard the warnings of Angie and Colson, but they held a shared understanding, an agreement, that they had little choice but to use whatever means they had to save the Origin, and give Island 7 a fighting chance at survival.

Cassie and Stitch nodded at Jay. Cassie drew Jay into a hug and turned on her heels, running for the exit. 'Be careful,' Cassie shouted over her shoulder. 'I'll contact you.' Then she was gone.

Chapter 18

Jay was keenly aware of Cassie's absence as they trekked north in search of the spark, the *Origin*. They'd be weaker without her combination of Given power and physical fighting ability. Without her, their fight would rely on the three of them, connecting with total trust and to their full potential.

The sun was high in the sky. The sandy surface over the rocks was dry and hard. On each side of the path, the vegetation looked parched. It reminded Jay of the heathland back home, where the shrubs always seemed to be trying to get as low to the ground as they could to stay out of the wind. Here, it was the heat that caused them to recoil.

'Fynbos,' Femi said from just behind Jay.

'Excuse me?'

'You were looking at the plants. We call this stuff Fynbos. This is Sandstone Fynbos.' He nodded towards the shrub-like plants that carpeted the floor for as far as Jay could see.

'What kind of a name is that?' Jay asked.

'Fynbos is a European name. It's Dutch I think, means "thin bush" or "fine bush" or something like that. Look.' He knelt to take the leaves of a shrub in his hand. Jay crouched with him. 'It has these thin leaves. They have adapted to the heat to minimise water loss.'

'Clever,' said Jay, leaning on Femi as she stood. Her knees and calves ached from the hill walking. She looked at the Fynbos, considering the power of pragmatism, of adapting to your surroundings, and to the dangers faced. Perhaps this was what she was doing by connecting not only to her Given power, but also to the Dark.

Femi stood. 'Many of the species here you won't find anywhere else.'

Jay looked across the landscape and tried to imagine what it would become if the Readers achieved their goal. 'You won't find them here either, if Atta gets his way.'

'Let's keep moving,' called Stitch from up ahead, his head skyward as he watched a buzzard circle above them.

'It's OK, Stitch,' Femi called after him, then smiled

at Jay. 'They won't feed on you unless you're already dead.'

As they neared the peak, Jay was surprised not to have encountered any Readers. She sensed an increasing darkness, and it brought mixed feelings. The connection to the Dark shown to her by Femi, and her ability to control it gave her confidence. But the challenge that lay somewhere on the other side of the peak, was something she could not underestimate. Atta had already gained the advantage.

'Time to bring in Angie?' said Stitch.

'Soon,' Jay said. 'It's a difficult connection to maintain, so the later, the better.'

At the peak, a rock formation stretched into the sky, providing shade from the sun on the east side and shelter from view. Jay, Stitch and Femi huddled in the shade, desperate for relief from the heat. Further east, they looked across a vast expanse of the flat top of the mountain, the green shrubbery interspersed with occasional collections of colour as flowers competed for space.

'There,' said Femi, pointing into the distance as he pulled his water bottle from his bag. 'People moving.'

Groups of people combed the mountain top like they were hunting for a missing person. They spread across the rocks in lines, picking their way through the vegetation. Darkness prickled inside Jay as she realised she had seen this image before – the mist, Readers, searching. The scene in front of her was that of the vision she had experienced back at the underground base with Tiago and Thabisa. Stitch moved to step closer but Jay pulled him back under the cover of the rocks.

'I thought they'd already found it,' said Stitch.

'Still looking,' said Jay. 'But it's here. I can feel it.'

Stitch nodded. 'What now?'

Jay searched her senses. She had no sense that Tiago or Annika's remains were anywhere near, and she'd not yet received anything from Cassie. Perhaps they'd been premature in their worry about the Readers finding the Origin.

Femi crouched then slumped down on the floor. 'We rest a minute.'

Jay joined him. 'We can get hold of Angie, and we can recharge before we go in fighting.' She totted up the number of Readers she could see. Four or five groups within her field of vision, maybe more on the other side of the ridge. Ten or twenty in each group.

Angie came through almost as soon as Jay leaned back and closed her eyes. Femi and Stitch both reached out and connected with Jay.

'You're there?' said Angie.

'We're at the top,' said Jay. 'There are Readers here.'

'I can feel them. And I can feel the power of the Given.'

'There's something I don't understand. There is no sign that they have the remains of Tiago and Annika. Cassie is heading down to the sink location to see if they've been moved.'

'Colson says we know nothing for certain. He thinks it is probably the remains that will destroy the Origin, but we don't know for sure.'

'What if they don't find the Origin?' Jay said.

Colson came through to her then, connected to Angie. 'Tell me what you feel, Jay?'

'What do you mean...' Jay started, but trailed off because she knew what Colson was asking. 'I feel like they've already found it. But they are still searching; I can see them with my own eyes.'

'You are sensing the inevitability. They are close, and in your power, you know that. Can you see the Origin?'

'No,' said Jay.

'Look below the surface,' said Colson. 'Beyond the physical.'

Jay opened further to the energy in the environment and scanned the mountaintop. Shimmers of light rippled across the surface like sonar, only to be deflected and dissolve into nothing when it reached the groups of Readers. She tried again. This time, a chink of white light escaped from the rocks on the southern edge of the mountaintop. She scanned again, feeling Stitch's hand tighten on her arm. Again, a white light emerged, and this time she focused in on it. The light punched through the surface as Jay allowed her power to wash over it, unearthing it like a long buried artefact.

'I see it,' she said. She drew back her power, afraid to expose the Origin's location to the Readers, but the Readers seemed oblivious.

'That's what you will need to defend from the Readers. If they find it, and they connect it with the remains of the Island's 8C and C, then the Origin will run dry of the energy needed to provide Given power.'

'We can never fight all these Readers,' said Jay.

'You might not have to,' Angie said, her words slow and deliberate, as if a thought was crystallising in her mind. 'All you need to do is stop the two elements coming together. Stop the remains coming into the location of the spark. You said Cassie was heading for the place they have Tiago?'

'If she finds them,' said Jay, 'then Cassie can get Tiago's remains well away, to somewhere they'll never be able to get to. But we don't know if she will already be too late.'

The images of Angie and Colson faded as Jay tried

to hold on to the connection. They stood. Jay took a step from cover. 'Wait!' Stitch said, his voice taught.

Jay and Femi stopped and turned. Jay strained her eyes to see what Stitch was looking at. In the distance, the groups of Readers had all stopped searching and had turned to look in Jay's direction, as if alerted to her presence.

They froze under the gaze of so many Readers; a shiver ran through Jay's bones. She shrivelled under the glare of their subversive power. Their energy was strong.

A single figure continued to move.

The hooded man shuffled around in the location where Jay had seen the Origin. She held her breath. As the three stared toward the hooded man, frozen under the icy glare of the other Readers, the man seemed to sense he was being watched and stopped, his head down.

Slowly, he turned in Jay's direction, and, even from distance she could see, sense, feel who this was. He pushed down his hood to reveal his face.

Atta.

CASSIE SLID down the last section of slope to the perimeter fence. She scrambled over to the post where the chain link still hung loose. She was out in the open, and her best chance of success was to act fast.

She pulled back the damaged fence and squeezed through. It sprung back behind her, catching her heel and drawing blood. She stifled a squeal with a hand slapped to her mouth. Scanning the open ground, she saw the little hut next to the prison building. Ignoring the pain in her heel, she dragged herself to stand and loped as fast as she could towards the hut.

The prison building was quiet. As she passed it, she looked at its door, open a jar. The front door of the hut next door was closed but not locked. It was as they'd left it, which surprised Cassie. If the remains of Tiago and Annika were so central to the destruction of the Origin, why leave it unguarded? She entered the building and closed the door, turning to peer through the crack of the frame to ensure no one had seen and followed her.

She tried to connect with Jay, but got nothing. Jay had been unresponsive since they'd parted company on the hill. She and Cassie had never perfected long distance connection, not like Jay and Stitch seemed to do with no effort, but she had at least expected to be able to connect to communicate a sense of what was happening.

Nothing. Except. Something. Someone...

Angie's image came to Cassie, its focus weak and

presence intermittent, but it was undoubtedly Angie. Cassie tried to relax and to clear her mind. She opened to allow Angie in to her consciousness.

'Cassie?' It was Angie's voice. 'Are you with Tiago's ashes?'

Cassie looked at where the wooden crate sat on a table. She sensed the remains of Tiago and Annika were still inside. 'Yes,' she said, then stepped towards the crate and rested a hand on the lid. She prised it open just enough to see that the two containers were there, then slammed it shut. 'They're both here.'

'Good,' said Angie. 'I have a message from Colson. Get their remains out of there, away from the Readers. If they don't have them, then they can't destroy the Origin.'

Cassie reached out to lift the crate, together with its contents. The crate was heavy and bulky, and the two containers would be too awkward for her to carry both at once. She turned back to the door, opening it a crack and scanning the yard. She was looking for a vehicle, something she could use to get away quickly with the crate. There were two Land Rovers parked next to the building opposite, and no sign of any Readers.

She slipped out of the hut and around to the back where she could follow the line of buildings around to where the Land Rovers sat, without breaking from cover. The last building was about fifty feet from the Land Rovers. She waited. Two Readers passed between the buildings on the far side, then nothing. With the crate in both her hands, she made a dash for the back of the nearest Land Rover and ducked around the side.

She waited.

Content that she'd not been seen, she peered up into the front of the vehicle and tried the handle.

Locked.

She moved around to the second vehicle and tried the handle. It opened, and she slipped inside, set the crate in the footwell and closed the door. She kept in the car so that she was out of sight of the front windows of the building next to the Land Rovers as she searched for the keys.

Nothing under the sun visor. Keys were always under the sun visor in the movies. She leaned towards the glove box when something caught her eye. A bunch of keys swinging from the ignition barrel.

She straightened in the driver's seat and clasped the keys, squeezing her foot gently on the accelerator pedal as she turned the ignition key. The engine fired with an unmuffled roar. She was sure the whole of the camp would come looking. Without waiting to find out, she slammed the Land Rover into reverse and crossed the yard so that the vehicle backed up against the hut.

Beyond the windscreen, a group of five Readers emerged from the building opposite. She looked over her shoulder at the wooden steps up to the wooden door of the hut. The floor of the hut was at about the same level as the back of the Land Rover. Speed would be her only friend. If she could just get the vehicle closer.

She pushed the Land Rover into first gear and pulled forward a few feet before crunching it back into reverse and slamming her foot down on the accelerator. She released the clutch, and the wheels spun for a few seconds before the vehicle lurched back towards the hut. As she made contact, she squeezed her eyes closed and braced herself. Her head snapped back against the headrest as the Land Rover slammed into the hut, wedging itself half way into the wooden building.

Cassie shook her head clear and clambered back through the Land Rover to where the box that contained Tiago and Annika sat on the table. She grabbed hold of the box and yanked it onto the floor and then into the back, securing it with a hook around the handle and onto the flat bed of the Land Rover so that it wouldn't fly out as she pulled away. Through the front, the Readers were already pulling at the door handles, trying to get to her. She lurched forward and pushed the lock down on the passenger door, but the driver's door was already open, a Reader reaching for her.

She kicked out, connecting her heel with the Reader's face and feeling the pain from where she'd sliced her heel on the fence earlier. The kick was enough to send the Reader tumbling, and for Cassie to slam and lock the door. Two more Readers made for the back of the vehicle but they'd have to climb through the wreckage of the hut before they could get there.

The engine stalled.

She turned the key and pushed the accelerator.

It whirred and died.

Again.

This time it caught, but died again.

Readers were in the hut now.

The engine caught. She revved it hard, black smoke pouring out the back. The gear box clunked, the wheels spun, and the vehicle lurched. The stairs of the hut fell away and the Reader at the back fell flat on his face. At the front, two Readers scattered, and a third was sent flying as Cassie struck him with a glancing blow of the front bumper. She didn't look back. She pushed her foot to the floor and powered towards the fence, not pausing to figure out if there was a more sensible exit route.

She ploughed into the fence, uprooting two of the metal fence posts and carrying the chain-mail fencing with the Land Rover for a hundred feet before it fell away and she could accelerate into the hills.

ATTA's Readers remained spread throughout the mountaintop, as if frozen in time, looking in Jay's direction. She couldn't be sure if the image of Atta before her was physical, or how he reached her in the blink of an eye, but the strength of his power was undeniable, and its signature clear.

A familiar and terrifying bitter taste seeped into the back of Jay's mouth. The sky darkened, and the wind whipped up. This was Atta at his strongest, in a land with a fully functioning tap into the core, overrun by Readers. Here he controlled the balance in his favour, and here he thrived.

He stood in silence, scrutinising Jay, ignoring Stitch and Femi as if they didn't exist.

The Readers in the background began to move. They collected in a single group and made towards the location of the Origin, surrounding the area so that Jay could no longer feel its presence amongst the waves of Dark energy.

'You found what you were looking for, then?' Jay said to Atta, trying to stop her voice from wobbling.

Her words seemed to snap him out of a trance, and

he looked her in the eye. As he did so, a pulse of Dark energy hit Jay and she staggered. Behind her, Stitch failed to stay upright and Femi had to catch his arm to prevent him toppling over the edge of the cliff.

'Yes,' said Atta, almost absently, as he looked from Jay to Stitch and Femi, then back again. 'We knew it was here somewhere,' he said, a frustration in his tone that reminded Jay how angry the world made Atta when he didn't easily get what he believed rightfully his. 'But it's the final pinpointing that is always difficult. We can't seem to home in on it. Always something in the way. It's as if the universe is trying to prevent the inevitable.' He smiled, a victorious, satisfied expression. 'Then you come to save the day.'

Jay's heart sunk at the implication that she, once again, had assisted this psychopath in his mission. Stitch gave away no sense that he knew what Atta was talking about. 'The source stone,' said Jay. 'That was the last time you trick us into anything.'

'Not quite,' he said, looking back over his shoulder as the Readers continued to swarm nearer the Origin. 'Your presence has once again been of value to me. The precise location could have alluded me for weeks, months. Who knows? But with your Given energy,' he said the word with disgust, 'it helps. You're like a little detector for the homing beacon. I mean, we would have found it anyway, eventually, but, you know, thanks.'

Behind Atta, the Readers continued digging. Sand and rock scattered and clouds of dust rose. Jay needed to catch her breath and gather her energy. She summoned strength from the ground below her, and from the intermittent ripples of energy that came over from the Origin. She thought about the darkness within her, tapping into it for a moment and then withdrawing. Her fear made her unsteady. In Atta's presence, her confidence waned.

Femi reached out for Jay through the power. She sensed his confidence and solidarity like a steadying hand on her back. He was with her, ready to fight to the end with her. His darkness, too, was clear. His power was tinged with a spark of energy from the Dark, and it felt strong. Stitch reached out to touch the back of Jay's arm, projecting his own energy through to Jay. She was not alone.

Atta's expression hardened, and Jay increased the energy to shield, to prevent him from interpreting their thoughts and intentions.

Jay gathered her energy and strengthened the connection with Femi and Stitch. She was about to launch an attack on Atta with everything they had when Stitch held her back. She glared at him.

'Thanks for taking out the source stone,' Atta said, his tone smug.

'It doesn't matter,' said Jay. 'You can't destroy the Origin.'

Atta laughed. 'You still don't get it? I don't need Tiago anymore. He has already given me what I need. I took from Annika half the power I need to destroy the Origin, and then from Tiago the other half. I don't need to ask permission. I took it from them, dragged it from their dead bodies. Bodies of the Given who you could not save. Now the power to take out the Origin is in me. All I need is the location of the Origin itself.' He grinned, and motioned over his shoulder to where the Readers closed in on Atta's prize.

'Why?' asked Jay, struggling for words and for options. Every route to their goal had been cut off, one by one, by Atta's carefully choreographed plans, of which Jay herself seemed to have played a starring role.

'Why what?' Atta said, a mix of confusion and annoyance in his face. 'My goal is the same as yours,' Atta said. 'Control. You might have evicted me from 8, but 7 is mine. The Given will not survive here. I have already won. And you will not get in my way again. This time you won't be around when I walk straight into 6, then 5.'

He grinned again, and Jay's anger fizzed beneath her skin. Gone were her doubts, her fears, her questions about which power to draw on and why. She knew what she wanted and was through dithering. She drew on Femi and Stitch, and on the power of the land, and released the pent up energy, directing it straight at Atta with all the strength she could gather.

FEMI AND STITCH pushed their own power through to Jay to reinforce her attack. White light emanated from Jay, increasing in its intensity until she could no longer see Atta, or the mountaintop.

She sensed Atta reeling in the face of her onslaught. Femi's darkness nipped at Jay, enticing her to use its strength to double up on the attack.

Atta was thrown from the hill, falling back over the cliff edge as Jay continued to direct the power into him, unrelenting. She sensed him hit the ground at the base of the cliff and still she continued to power her attack into him.

After a minute, Stitch and Femi pulled back their power, but Jay continued. Stitch put a hand on Jay's arm, releasing her from her focus. She eased back her attack until the white light faded and the dust settled. Together the three of them stepped towards the edge of the cliff and looked over, expecting to see Atta's body prone at the foot of the cliff.

He was gone.

'Did we kill him?' asked Stitch.

'No,' said Femi. 'I can feel him. He's strong.'

Jay turned away from Femi and Stitch and back to the Readers. They continued to excavate, apparently oblivious to their battle with Atta. 'Help me with these Readers.' As she spoke, Jay slid quickly down the slope and took off towards the Readers. Her energy levels were high. The attack on Atta gave her confidence, and the power of the Origin was palpable. As she ran, the vegetation beneath her feet seemed to push her along. With each footfall, the green leaves of the Fynbos stretched, grew, and cushioned her. The wind whipped across the flat top of the mountain, cooling her face.

Over her shoulder, Femi and Stitch kept pace. As they approached the swarm of Readers, vines and roots beneath the ground broke the surface. Twisting roots curled around the legs and torsos of Readers, pulling them to the ground. Jay pushed herself into the throng and white light once more rained down on them, expanding out from the three of them. More roots and vines burst through the rocks and pulled Readers to the floor, dragging them further into the ground. Readers disappeared as their bodies dissolved under the power of the environment, fed by the channelling of energy from the Origin.

A guttural scream rained down from above their heads, knocking Jay's concentration. A second roar came, and dark clouds descended.

Atta had returned.

Vines shrivelled, and the vegetation around the stumbling Readers receded. Atta's image appeared in the centre of the throng. Jay, Stitch and Femi froze. Jay gasped for breath, exhausted by the fight with the Readers. The remaining Readers gradually re-grouped, standing with Atta, facing the three Given.

With another scream of anger and defiance, Atta attacked.

The lightness in Jay, Stitch and Femi went dark. Jay's vision blurred, and then it was gone - she was blind. She was so weak, her energy sapped to the point that her senses began to collapse. The wind that previously seemed to support them now turned, sucking the dust up into the air and spinning it around Jay like a mini tornado. The blackness became deepened by the swirling dust – clogging their eyes. The noise pounded at their ears. Jay tried to gather whatever power she had left to shield them, but it made no difference.

Pain in her legs, her arms, and then in her head. She lifted her hands to the sides of her head as Atta and his Readers raised the level of their attack. She saw nothing but blackness, heard nothing but the roar of the wind in her ears.

Stitch?

Femi?

The roar in her ears turned to the screams of Femi and Stitch. Her legs wobbled and gave way. She was sliding, with a scuttle of stones and sand, down, down a slope. Head over foot.

She felt a hand on her wrist. She reached out and held onto Femi.

Then there was nothing. The noise was gone, leaving nothing but a ringing in her ears. She and Femi had come to a stop at the foot of a slope. Her eyes were caked. She blinked, and tears washed away the dust.

The dust settled. No sign of Atta or Readers.

'Jay?' Stitch called from just a few feet away, buried in the sandy slope. He pulled himself free and dragged his body over to where Jay and Femi were catching their breath. Jay scanned her body for damage, feeling nothing serious but total exhaustion and an absence of Given power.

'Look,' Femi said, pointing up to the top of the slope.

Atta was there, stood over the location that Jay knew to be the Origin. The Readers had moved away to give Atta the access he wanted. As Jay, Femi and Stitch looked on, Atta opened his arms and released a stream of dark energy into the ground at the Origin.

WHITE LIGHT EXPLODED from the ground in front of Atta. Jay shielded her eyes. The light enveloped Atta and the Readers, some Readers staggering away, their arms covering their eyes. For a moment, Jay wondered if the Origin was resisting Atta's attack, pushing back with the great force of power contained within. But Atta remained solid, pushing his own power into the Origin with no obvious resistance. It was as if the action of Atta's attack had cracked open the Origin, and now its energy was leaking away into the atmosphere where it could no longer form the source of Given power.

As the light from the Origin faded, darkness gathered like an early dusk. The heat from the sun was shielded by gathering clouds. The last of the white energy fizzled and died, and Jay felt empty. A vacuum spread from her chest through to the extremities of her limbs, and it was like she felt when she lost Alf, when his life slipped away.

Stitch flopped to the ground, all energy gone.

Femi looked from Jay to Stitch and back to Atta. Jay felt his anger. He too had been weakened by the loss of Given energy, but he was defiant. He pulled himself to stand as if readying to attack.

Jay could barely summon the strength to speak. 'It's over,' she whispered.

Atta dragged his attention from whatever remained of the Origin. In a split second he was with them, in Femi's face. Femi swung at him, at the same time as attacking with his power. Atta resisted his blow without moving, using his own Dark power to throw Femi to the floor. He grabbed him by the collar and pulled him to stand, Femi's hands pinned to his sides by the force of Atta's power. 'You dare use my power against me?' he said.

Femi's expression remained firm. Jay sensed his rising anger, drawing his dark energy through his body. She felt her own wisps of darkness pulling together to help keep Jay on her feet. 'Femi,' said Jay. 'Don't.'

Femi snapped his head to look at Jay. She felt his anger at everything – at her, Atta, the Universe.

Atta laughed, reading Femi. 'She'll never use the darkness against us,' he said. 'And neither will you.' He raised his hand to bring down the full force of his power on Femi.

'Stop!' Jay shouted with as much as she had in her. 'Let these two go. They are of no threat to you. Take me. I'll do what you want.'

Atta paused a moment. He smiled. Jay knew that he'd respond to her admission that he had won. Femi backed off, stumbling away from Atta and back towards Stitch. Jay caught Femi's eye and sent a flick of her eye towards the cliff and the waterfall below. This would be the only way out for Femi and Stitch.

'Why would I do that?' said Atta. 'I already have all three of you. There's not an ounce of power between you. The last thing I'm going to do is let any of you go, to crawl off somewhere to recharge. No, we end this right here.'

Jay stepped between Atta and where Femi was helping Stitch to his feet. She waved Femi on as she squared up to Atta. Her Given energy was absent, dissolved into the air with the loss of power from the Origin. She connected with the dark power that still resided inside, and prepared to protect Femi and Stitch for as long as it took for them to get away. 'Go,' she urged Femi.

As Atta took a step towards her, Jay released all the darkness she held in her heart. Atta faltered, probably more out of surprise than from the force of Jay's attack, but it was long enough for Femi to drag Stitch to the edge and launch both of them over and into the flow of the waterfall. Atta staggered to the edge, looking into the spray for signs of Femi and Stitch. 'Idiot,' he said, turning back to Jay, who had slumped to her knees in exhaustion. 'They won't survive that fall.'

Jay knew Stitch couldn't swim. She just prayed that Femi would find him before he slipped to the bottom of whatever pool was at the foot of the cliff. Atta turned once more to peer over the cliff, as if he expected Femi and Stitch to come into view. With his back turned, Jay thrust herself to her feet and launched towards him. He turned just in time to see her coming as she knocked him out of her way and threw herself after her friends.

Chapter 19

In a clearing just back from the edge of the river, Cassie put the finishing touches to the shallow graves of Tiago and Annika.

She had driven deep into the wooded region in the foothills of the mountains, taking the Land Rover off-road and clawing her way as far as she could, until she hit the river. She figured this was deep enough, remote enough to be hidden from hunting Readers. The bodies of Tiago and Annika wouldn't fall into the hands of the darkness.

'There,' she said aloud, standing and brushing the sand and silt from her hands. She hadn't known Annika, but Tiago was a good man, and she felt for his family. She felt Thabisa's devastation.

She pushed her way through the bushes and back to the shore of the river, where the Land Rover stood on the sand, its back doors hanging off their hinges from when she had reversed into the building back at the camp. The crate that had been their coffin lay in pieces on the floor next to the vehicle. She flung each separate piece of wood into the water and watched it float downstream, picking up speed as it caught the main current and turned the corner. Looking back up into the hills, she thought about Jay. She'd felt waves of activity from her and Stitch before she entered the woods, but now all was quiet.

She stepped into the shallows to wash her hands, wipe away the sense of death from the remains of Tiago and Annika, as well as the grime from digging with her hands. She splashed water onto her face and stood, sensing an energy flowing with the river, down from the mountains. In the distance, a spark of light flickered in the hills, like a piece of glass catching the sunlight.

A wave of energy pushed her back like a gust of wind. The spark of light erupted at the top of the mountain, streaming into the sky. It was a beautiful sight, but with the light came an overwhelming sense of darkness. In the shallow water, Cassie fell to her knees under the weight of Dark energy. 'Jay,' she whispered, unable to drag her eyes away from the light as it faded, like a spent firework.

In less than a minute, the light was gone, and with

it, the sense of all power of the Given. Cassie's body felt heavy and weak. Her limbs were rubber. She pulled herself out of the water and inspected her hands, a light tingling feeling spreading through her fingers as if her energy was seeping away and into the air.

'Jay,' she whispered once more. Was she dead? This vacuum of Given power, did it mean that Jay was dead?

The answer was obvious to Cassie. She knew what she was feeling: it was the Origin. The spark of Given power has been destroyed. But how? Tiago and Annika are here. They must have found another way.

Cassie put her hands to her head and paced the little beach in front of the Land Rover. She opened to the energy but got nothing, not a wisp of power. Everything was gone. If Jay was alive, there was no way she could reach her. There was no means of communication without the power.

If Jay and Stitch were alive, by now they'd be on the run. Her best option was to get somewhere safe where Jay would go. The source at the confluence of rivers would be useless, benign. The realisation then hit Cassie that they could not transport back home through the source at the crater lake. Their route home had also been taken.

'The underground,' she said under her breath. The

only place left where Jay would go. And the same place to which the Readers would surely be heading. She jumped in the driver's seat of the Land Rover and fired the engine, wheel spinning away heading south, to follow the river back into Kaapstown.

Jay's lungs were bursting.

Her head spun from the force at which she hit the water.

She couldn't tell which way was up.

It had felt like hours she'd been under the water.

There were no whispers through the water of the unnamed river, no tendrils of support to push Jay up and in the direction of the surface.

At last, she broke through the surface. Air streamed into her lungs as the water coughed up. She gasped. More water pounded her from above. She was under the waterfall, the noise of the water hammering down all around her.

She took a deep breath and pushed herself through the water, away from the waterfall. She did not know how far she was from the edge, but she knew she'd not be able to swim for long. Her body ached. Her chest wheezed with the effort. She imagined herself drifting back below the surface as she swam. The battering from above seemed never ending. The image of Stitch in her mind pushed her on. He would need her. He hated swimming. Hated the water.

Then she was clear.

The torrent abated, and the vista opened up before her. She was clear of the waterfall, and a short swim from the edge of the pool. Treading water for a moment to catch her breath, she edged further from the waterfall and out of the fine spray that came across the surface of the water in gusts.

She spotted Femi on the near shore, carrying a heavy sack. He laid it on the sand. 'Stitch!'

She gasped and sucked in water, then coughed, managing to only just keep her head above water. Femi leaned over Stitch as he lay on his back. Jay started to swim with all her remaining energy. She kept her eyes open and on Femi and Stitch. He lifted Stitch and turned him, laying him over his lap. Then he whacked him on the back. Three times he hit Stitch.

Jay went under. Mouth full of water. Coughing. Eyes stinging as she tried to force them open to see Stitch and Femi as she resumed swimming.

Stitch on his side. Femi over him.

Jay reached the shore and scrambled out of the water on her hands and knees, her strength giving way twice so that her face landed in the sand. At last, she was on her feet. Femi saw her and put up a hand to signal where he was but Jay was already running towards him.

She skidded to a halt at Stitch's side and almost slammed into him. His eyes were closed. He wasn't moving.

'Stitch!'

'He's OK,' said Femi, a hand on Jay's shoulder. 'Go easy.'

'Stitch?' Jay said again, not taking Femi's word for it. She leaned down and took his face in her hands. She whispered his name and his eyes fluttered and opened. She pulled his head onto her lap and breathed in the relief, looking up into the sky.

'It's OK,' said Femi, his expression one of concern for Jay rather than Stitch.

Stitch raised himself up to sit. The three of them sat in silence for a few minutes, like washed up debris on the shore.

Stitch slung an arm around Jay and pulled her to him. 'I'm OK,' he whispered into her ear. Warm tears rolled down Jay's cheeks. When they pulled apart, Stitch turned to Femi and slapped a hand on his back. 'Thanks, man.'

'I'm just glad it didn't come to a need for the kiss of life. Might have drawn the line there.' He smiled.

Jay wiped her eyes and gathered herself. There was no time to feel sorry for herself about their epic failure to stop Atta. Now it was a matter of survival. The chances of getting themselves off the Island with their lives seemed slim. And there were still other Given who would look to Jay for answers. 'There's no power,' she said. 'Nothing.'

Stitch shook his head. 'Feels weird. I've not felt this weak since before I first got my mark.'

Jay knew the feeling Stitch described. She couldn't recall a time when she'd felt an absence of Given energy. For as long as she could remember, there had always been something.

'There's still the Dark energy,' Femi said, his voice tentative, as if suggesting something underhand.

Jay looked up at the mountaintop. She had no sense of Atta. 'I can't feel him.'

She looked at Femi for confirmation and he shook his head. 'They either think we're dead, or they think we don't matter. With no power, we are little threat to him now.'

'We are done,' said Stitch. 'We can't get home.'

Jay and Femi exchanged a glance. Stitch was right. Without the power, there would be no way of getting away through the source at the crater lake. And the power of the Readers would be so dominant that any fight would be futile.

'They'll be looking to finish us,' said Stitch.

'We need to get off this Island,' said Jay.

'How?' said Stitch.

Jay looked at Femi for answers. 'The boats,' he said.

Jay nodded. 'The underground. We can take the boats. We can take all the remaining Given and get as far away from here as we can.'

Thabisa had shown Jay the boats in the depths of the underground. There was an escape route that led out into the bay. If they could keep the Readers away for long enough, they might be able to get everyone out.

'It will be a miracle if we get off this island,' said Stitch. 'There is no source. No power. And the Readers are probably already at the underground. Where do you think Atta is heading if he's not up there? And we can't even contact Thabisa...'

'Stitch,' Femi said. 'Calm down. One step at a time.' He turned to Jay. 'What about Cassie?'

Jay had already thought of Cassie. She was sure that Cassie would also head for the underground. There was no other sensible option. 'She'll catch up with us.'

Femi stood and made his way towards the tree line. 'We can take the river,' he said.

Jay looked back at the river, powering downstream to where it would meet the crater lake. Femi's plan to use the river was a good one. They'd get to the crater lake in a much shorter time than if they tried to travel over ground. 'All the way to the City?'

'No,' said Femi as he dragged a piece of wood from the trees. He dumped it on the ground with frustration. 'If we can find something to float on, then this river will take us as far as the divergence at North Ridge. There's a tributary that will lead us straight through to the underground. That's the section of river that will take the boats out into the bay. But we can't take it all the way into the underground because it is not passable. We have to get out and make the last section by land. A mile or so around to the entrance to the underground.'

Jay nodded.

'Why don't we use that?' Stitch said. Jay looked over to see that Stitch was pointing at the remains of a dilapidated-looking row boat upturned just inside the tree line.

Femi made his way over to it and turned it upright. Jay and Stitch joined him as he slotted a side panel back into place. 'Might work,' he said with a smile.

THE OLD BOAT HELD TOGETHER, and mostly, the river was calm, only speeding through sections where it narrowed and meandered around rocky outcrops. Jay and Femi guided the boat with makeshift oars fashioned from discarded planks of wood. The afternoon sun burned off the moisture in their clothes, leaving Jay mostly dry but for sodden wet shoes in the bottom of the boat.

'There,' said Femi, pointing his oar at a divergence of the river to a small tributary. 'Row on your side.'

Jay plunged her oar deep and pulled the boat around. They slid into the stream of flow that took them out of the main river and on the path of its tributary.

'This is tiny,' Stitch said as they left the main river behind, the bottom of the boat scraping occasionally on the bed of the stream. They drifted for a few minutes, with Jay and Femi now and again pushing them forward with their oars. The stream narrowed further and deepened slightly, giving them a little more momentum as they sped up through the section where hills gave way to fields, and then to low-rise buildings on the outskirts of the City.

It was quiet as they drifted through the City. Even the dipping of their oars into the water seemed like a disturbance of the silence. They allowed the boat to drift naturally towards the southern edge of the City. 'Not far now,' said Femi.

Jay leaned back and took a moment to rest and recharge. There was no power in the river, the land or the nearby sea. No whispers. No comforting sense of being supported. Kaapstown felt drained of all life.

The river became shallow so that the boat scraped

the bottom in places. After a few more minutes, the water dried up completely so that there was nothing but a gentle trickle of the stream as it disappeared into the rocks. The boat ground to a halt. 'This is as far as we go,' said Femi, standing. 'We are close. We just need to get around to the entrance to the underground.'

Jay and Stitch stood, stepping out of the boat and into the shallow water, before climbing up the slope of the bank to a towpath. A waft of stagnant water followed them from the dry riverbed. Along the towpath, the vegetation wilted. Overhanging trees weighed heavy, drooping towards the path as if too tired to hold themselves up. Jay reached and took a leaf into her hand and it came away from its branch at the slightest of touches.

'The environment here has been suffering, even before they killed the Origin. Now everything will die.'

Jay's heart ached for what was to become of Island 7. As she turned back to the tree, she saw that many of its leaves had already fallen, and a darkness seemed to spread through its branches from its trunk and from deeper under the ground. She was reminded of Alf and Colson's interpretation of the literature on the Event in their history that followed a period of deterioration of the environment. On Island 4, before the successful destruction of the dark core, that Island suffered from being overrun by the darkness, and the impact was something like Jay could see in these trees.

A sound came from somewhere behind them. Stitch and Femi were a way ahead, already at the next corner. There was nothing but the sound of her own blood pumping in her ears. The silence was eerie. She looked up into the trees, hoping for something – a bird at least, but there was nothing. She hurried after Stitch, keeping an eye over her shoulder for whatever made a noise, but seeing nothing.

She bumped into the back of Stitch as she rounded the corner and faced Femi and Stitch staking out the entrance to the underground. 'What?' asked Jay.

'There's a Land Rover there.'

By the hidden entrance, a Land Rover, like those used by the Readers was parked up, its front door open like someone had piled out in a hurry. The back doors of the Land Rover hung limply by their hinges, like they'd been ripped off in an accident.

'It's quiet,' said Jay. 'Let's go.' She moved from cover and made for the bushes at the end of the under-pass where there was a concealed entrance to the back route in to the underground. Stitch followed. Femi hesitated a moment before scurrying after them.

Before Jay pushed her way through the bushes, someone called to her. 'Wait,' came a familiar voice.

It was Cassie.

She ran to Jay from the other side of the road, enveloping her in a hug. 'Hey, Cass.'

'I thought I'd lost you guys.' Cassie released Jay and pulled Stitch into a hug. 'Seriously, thought you were dead. I couldn't feel anyone. Nothing.'

Femi nodded to Cassie, and she acknowledged him without seeing the need for another hug.

'The power is dead,' said Stitch.

Cassie hesitated a moment before saying, 'The Origin? They destroyed it? I thought so.'

'What happened to Tiago? And my mother?' asked Femi.

'I made sure they had an honourable burial,' said Cassie.

'Thank you,' said Femi. 'Now we need to move.'

He made to head to the entrance but Cassie stopped him. 'Wait. We can't go in there.'

'Why?' said Jay.

'I've been in. There are Readers everywhere. They're rounding up the Given. They have Thabisa.'

THEY EDGED down the tunnel towards the deep caverns. Shouts and screams echoed from the depths. Jay sensed energy in the caves and for a moment dared to hope there might be a flicker of Given power remaining. Femi seemed to read her thoughts, and, catching her eye, shook his head. 'It's not Given energy you feel.'

They reached the corridor to the main cavern, where the pathway split into two, one leading deeper into the tunnels below, and one heading directly into the hall where Jay had first met Femi and the rest of the Given. 'You two go down,' Jay said to Femi and Cassie. 'Me and Stitch will take this level.'

'No,' said Femi. 'We stick together. We don't have the power. If we split, we will be weaker. This will be a physical fight, and we need to have each other's backs.'

'He's right,' said Cassie.

Jay nodded. She knew they were right. It was an uncomfortable feeling to go into a fight with Readers without the protection of Given power.

'And remember what I said,' said Femi. 'We still have some power to draw on.'

Jay nodded again. 'How many Given are holed up here altogether?'

'Less than twenty.'

Jay stepped forward towards the main cavern where the shouting grew louder, and she thought she heard Thabisa's voice. Cassie stepped ahead of Jay, taking the lead. In a physical fight, Cassie was the best Jay knew, and she felt safe to have her by her side.

At the main entrance, they waited a moment,

watching from the cover of the passageway. The Readers had guns, shoving the Given against the back wall of the cavern and forcing them to the floor, facing the wall. Jay counted six Given. Thabisa was there with Enzo. One of the Readers had Enzo by the arm and flung her to the floor next to Thabisa. Thabisa turned on him but it was a mistake. The butt of his rifle came down on the side of her face before she could utter more than a grunt of derision. She went down, Enzo shielding her from any more blows. The Reader backed off and Thabisa nursed a cut to her cheek.

Femi flushed red with rage and lurched to enter the cavern. Cassie and Jay held him back. 'Wait,' said Jay.

'I'll kill them,' Femi said through gritted teeth.

There were just three Readers in the room, all with their backs to Jay and her friends, their guns hanging over their shoulders. Jay motioned for Femi and Stitch to move, but silently, so they could take the Readers by surprise. The last thing they wanted was for one of those guns to go off with all the Given in the room. Jay and Cassie moved too, towards the nearest Reader.

With the briefest of glances between them, they jumped the Readers from behind. Jay reached for the gun, wrestling it away from danger, before thrusting a knee into the Reader and an elbow to his face. As he hit the floor, Thabisa was there, ready to pile into him.

Jay held her back as another Given took the gun and pointed it at the Reader.

Femi and Stitch had another Reader up against the wall, his gun in his back. Cassie's victim was unconscious on the floor. As Thabisa turned to Jay, three more Readers entered the room. They were quickly overpowered by a group of Given, and they too were lined up at gunpoint.

Thabisa looked to Jay, the questions clear in her eyes.

'We failed. The Origin is dead,' said Jay. 'There's nothing left but to get out of here before Atta turns up and kills us all.'

A sadness descended through Thabisa's eyes – a confirmation that this was the end of her time in Kaapstown. But she was not surprised. She had already known that the Given power had been extinguished. 'We have to get to the boats,' she said. 'But there are so many Readers here. They are everywhere, turning things upside down on the lower levels.'

'Looking for something?'

'No,' said Thabisa. 'Only rooting out the Given. They want all of us, either dead or transformed to Reader is my guess.'

'How many are missing?' asked Jay.

Thabisa scanned the room, counting her friends.

'At least six. Probably they are in the residential section. They will know to head down to the boats.'

They tied up the Readers and secured them in the adjacent cavern as the Given readied themselves to head down into the tunnels.

'We leave no one,' said Thabisa. Jay nodded, and they split into two groups. Thabisa took one group through the west passages whilst Jay, Stitch, Femi and Cassie took the east. They would work their way down to the boats and pick up any Given not yet heading that way.

The passages interconnected like a rabbit warren, with multiple branches and routes leading to the same place. Jay led the way. She picked up speed and soon they were running through the tunnels. A Reader stepped into Jay's path and she threw her body into him, cracking him back against the cave wall. She didn't wait to see him slip to the floor. At the next branch, they split. Readers came from all directions. Jay and Cassie worked as a pair, Stitch and Femi out of sight.

Two Readers overpowered Cassie, a gun wedged up under her chin. Jay turned to help, but took a blow to the head. Two readers stood over her. She tried to stand, but they had already opened to their power and pushed their darkness into Jay's mind. She raised her hands to the sides of her head, the pain blinding her. White light filled her head.

In a heartbeat, Jay was free. The Readers slammed back into the wall and slipped to the floor. She looked up to see Femi reaching out a hand. She felt the darkness flowing from his body. The Readers were both out of it, knocked unconscious by Femi's manipulation of their own dark energy. Femi pulled Jay to stand and turned to help Cassie, who was battling with two Readers.

Femi pulled one of the Readers off Cassie and sent him to the floor as Cassie swung a high kick at the other. They both lay unmoving at Cassie's feet. 'Where's Stitch?' said Jay. Cassie and Femi turned as Stitch appeared behind them, a dazed expression and his hair spiked at the side like he'd just got out of bed. Jay scanned him for damage, running her hands down his arms and half expecting to find a bullet wound.

'Hey now, mind those hands,' Stitch said, brushing her off, a sarcastic grin.

They pushed deeper into the underground, trying to stick together. Readers came in groups of three or four, so as long as they kept tight, they fended them off easily enough. The tunnels didn't allow Readers to spot them from distance in time to use their powers, so as long as they continued to use stealth, they had an advantage. They found no more Given until they reached the second-lowest level.

A cavern widened almost to the size of the main cavern on the upper levels. Jay edged towards its entrance, hearing a now familiar sound of Readers issuing instructions to the Given under gunpoint. Peering around the side of the cave wall, she saw that a group of six Readers had two Given under gunpoint, instructing them towards the east steps that would take them back up to the higher levels. One of them was Sanata, friend of Thabisa.

'We can take them,' said Cassie. But as soon as she'd said these words, three more Readers appeared in the tunnel behind them. The nearest raised his rifle, but Femi was on him like a shot, with Stitch just behind. Stitch lunged for the second Reader's gun as he raised it at Femi. A shot rang out, the bullet ricocheting off the walls as the Reader hit the floor under Stitch's attack. The third Reader was too far away for Cassie or Jay to reach him before he raised his gun at Cassie.

Cassie froze. Stitch and Femi were both on the floor, grappling with the other two Readers. Time seemed to slow as Jay watched the Reader's rifle level up and settle on Cassie, his finger on the trigger. She opened her mouth to scream but nothing came out. A stirring of darkness passed through Jay and she opened to it. It flowed from her chest, in the same way as the Given power. Time slowed some more and Jay's energy grew, streaming from her chest through to her arms, hands, fingers. The pent up scream exploded from Jay's lips, and a torrent of darkness powered towards the Reader as he squeezed the trigger.

The bullet released, the gun kicked back, but Jay's power battered into the Reader, his gun, and the bullet, washing them back into the tunnel in a blast of dust and light.

Femi and Stitch staggered to their feet as the Readers retreated down the tunnel. Jay's eyes were wide, her jaw open as she stared down the tunnel after the retreating Readers. Femi grinned. 'That's what I'm talking about,' he said, then stepped past her and into the cavern.

The cavern was empty. With Jay and her friends distracted, the Readers had already moved off with their captives. Femi nudged Cassie. 'Me and you. We can head up after them.' Cassie nodded. 'Jay, you and Stitch keep going. And don't look so shell-shocked.' He smiled but Jay still couldn't get it together. She'd not felt that level of strength of power of the darkness before. At least not since... the Event. But even then, it was a combination of dark and light. A flutter of hysteria rose through her body and she had to stop herself from smiling at the thought of what she'd just done. Yes, Femi had told her. And, yes, Stitch has tried to get it through to her. But, she never really believed the sacrifice of Given purity was worth the ability to make use of the darkness. Until she felt what she just felt. That was power to rival the strongest of her Given power.

Femi grabbed Jay by the shoulders and shook her from her trance. 'Go!' he said. 'You can dwell on it all later.' And, with that, Femi and Cassie turned to head back up through the tunnels.

JAY AND STITCH came to the top of a set of steps carved out in the rock. The sound of rushing water filled the tunnels below. They exchanged a glance. They must be close to where the river flowed through the underground and out into the bay. Stitch led the way as they pressed on.

At the foot of the steps, they emerged into a great open cave that framed a vast expanse of blue sky. The sea lapped at a beach beneath the grand arch of the roof of the cave. On the far side, a waterfall burst through the rocks and flowed out into the bay.

Boats, four of them, big enough to carry fifty people on each, were moored up against the river bank on the far side. At the nearest boat, Thabisa was helping people onto the deck. She looked up, and seeing Jay and Stitch, raised a hand. Jay jumped down onto the sand by the shore and made towards the boats.

Thabisa met them half way. 'Everyone here?' asked Jay.

'Most,' said Thabisa. 'Five missing. Three are dead.' Her face was grave.

'Femi and Cassie have gone after two Given. Sanata was one of them.'

Thabisa's expression brightened at the knowledge her friend was alive. 'So that's everyone accounted for,' she said.

'Where's Enzo?' asked Jay. Thabisa turned and motioned towards the boat. Enzo was on board, leaning over the railing on the deck.

'I guess we take just one boat?' said Jay.

Thabisa nodded. 'The others we will leave moored, in case there are more of the Given who eventually make their way here in time.'

To their left, Readers poured from a passageway in the rocks. Shots rang out. Thabisa looked up at Enzo and moved to make a dash for the boat, but more shots came, pinging off the rocks. 'Wait,' Jay shouted, turning to get a look at how many they were up against. Their cover was positioned between the Readers and the boat, so the Readers would have to go through them to get to the Given on the boat.

'Look,' Thabisa said, nodding towards the Reader at the front of the group of some eight or ten Readers.

It was the Reader who had killed Tiago. Thabisa's face hardened. Again she made to move, this time in the direction of the Readers, and again Jay held her back. 'Not the time,' Jay said. 'We're too outnumbered.'

The Readers held their position, content to wait it out. Jay thought of Atta. He would be on his way if he was not here already. She couldn't imagine Atta allowing his Readers to finish off the underground sanctuary of the Given without him. He took joy in the destruction of the Given.

Thabisa made a signal to Enzo on deck, something that Enzo immediately understood, and she disappeared from view. 'What was that?' asked Stitch.

'I told her to prepare to leave.' She paused a moment, looking at the space vacated by Enzo. 'She has power developing, I'm sure of it. She still gets something from that stone, the pendant. She won't let it out of her sight. It's like it's all she had left of her father. She connects with it, even after it lost its shine when the source stone was destroyed.'

'We need to wait for Cassie and Femi, with Sanata,' said Jay.

'We will wait as long as it is safe to wait,' said Thabisa.

Stitch nudged Jay. 'You know what you need to do,' he said.

Jay nodded. She was already exploring her inner darkness, but struggled to feel how to control and manage it. It had escaped her in anger when Cassie faced imminent danger. Would she have to be under direct attack before she can use it? Wisps of energy came to her, rippling through her chest. As the Readers were upon them, Jay readied to stand, to do whatever she could to hold them off.

Shots rang out.

The Readers scattered as gunshots pinged off the rocks, coming from the passageway at the cliff face. It was Cassie and Femi. Followed by Sanata and another man. Cassie waved a rifle in front of her, bullets peppering the sand before the Readers. Jay and Stitch crouched closer to Thabisa to stay well out of Cassie's firing line. Three of the Readers scrambled past Jay and away to the cover of the tunnels. The next to come around the side of the rocks was Tiago's killer. Thabisa thrust out her leg and the Reader flew into the sand in front of her.

She stood over him, and he turned onto his back to face her. He moved to stand but Thabisa kicked out at him, connecting her boot with his chin so that his head snapped back and hit the sand. He groaned. Thabisa crouched over him, her face screwed up in anger. He raised his head again and Thabisa smacked him with the heel of her hand. Stitch made to stand but Jay put a hand out. 'Leave it. This is personal.'

Femi and Cassie rounded the corner, Cassie with the rifle comfortable in her hands as if she'd been born holding it. The remaining Readers scattered to the cover of the rocks. 'We had better get moving. They won't remain hidden for long,' said Femi.

Sanata approached Thabisa as she delivered another blow to the Reader, knocking him unconscious. 'Hey,' Sanata said, her tone gentle. 'Let's move.'

Thabisa dragged herself away from the Reader, her expression manic. She looked up towards the boat, searching for her little girl. Enzo was below deck, and Jay felt relief that the child had not had to witness her mother's act of violence.

'Is that everyone?' asked Cassie.

'Everyone who is still alive. Any signs of Atta?'

Cassie shook her head but Femi said, 'I can feel him.' He paused a moment. 'I think we can keep him away,' he said. 'I have been working on the shield, like a barrier, but I need your help. You think you can do it?'

Jay nodded. She, too, felt the Dark presence rising and the chance of another encounter felt almost inevitable.

Femi raised his eyebrows. 'He's here,' he said.

A gust of wind pushed through the cavern and Jay

felt the Dark creep around her body as if weakening her bones. 'Cassie. Go with Thabisa. Make sure they all get on the boat. Don't wait for us.'

'But–' Cassie started, pointing her gun towards the main entrance to the cavern.

'Please, Cassie. We need to make sure everyone is clear.'

Cassie turned, reluctantly following the others. Stitch stood next to Jay. 'I'm staying,' he said.

'I know you are,' said Jay. 'I need you to do something for me.'

A stronger gust of wind picked up the dry sand and whipped it around Jay, Femi, and Stitch. Jay shielded her eyes as the sand battered against her. As the whirling sand settled, Atta appeared in the entrance to the cavern, less than two hundred feet away.

'Here we go,' said Stitch. 'Are we ready this time?'

Jay reached deep inside her. She felt the power of the darkness. It still scared her, but not in the same way as when it seemed to her to be in direct conflict with her innate Given power. Now, the Dark energy was free, without ambiguity, and her aim was clear. She needed to connect with her darkness for the survival of the Given. Atta may have the upper hand in the control of Island 7, but he would not take the Given with him. They would not succumb to his plan to transform or kill all the Given in this land. 'You feel it, Stitch,' she said. 'The darkness inside?'

Stitch closed his eyes as if he'd thought Jay would never ask. He had tried to persuade Jay to explore the darkness with him on countless occasions, and she'd knocked him down. Now she needed him to embrace it, to connect with her and Femi, and defend the passage of this boat from Kaapstown.

'If we do this,' said Femi. 'We won't have long. We won't be able to hold him forever.'

'Just long enough for them to get free,' said Jay. She wasn't sure what was coming, but whatever it was, it was coming fast. As her anger and determination to protect the Given reached its peak, a shimmer appeared in the air between her and Atta. Femi and Stitch saw it, felt it, and progressed to channel their own power into the barrier that was forming between them. They may not be able to attack him directly with the dark energy, but they could create a barrier – a shield to contain the danger, at least for a time.

Femi turned to Jay, and he smiled. Jay felt his power build and flow into the barrier. Stitch, too, had a smile on his face. The flow of darkness through the ground and into Jay's body felt as natural as if it were the power of the Given.

The shield continued to grow until it reached the roof of the cave, completely separating Atta from his target. 'He's coming,' said Stitch as Atta picked up speed, heading towards them across the rocks flanked by Readers. More Readers poured into the cave.

Jay looked back at the boat, still moored at the side of the cave. 'Why aren't they leaving?'

Atta halved the distance between them in a few seconds. 'More!' Shouted Femi. 'We need more in the barrier. Keep going.'

Jay and Stitch moved closer together, continuing to focus on the barrier. Femi moved in until the three were physically connected. As Femi joined, their energy flowed freely. The shimmer became an opaque shield just as Atta smashed into it. The barrier rocked, shaking the cave from the beach through to the arched roof. Atta rebounded and lay motionless on the rocks. Readers continued to pile into the barrier, each rebounding with equal force.

Stitch laughed. A hysterical relief.

'Stitch!' Jay said. 'Concentrate. We haven't won yet.'

Femi looked across at Jay, and she knew they were thinking the same thing. With a final push of the Dark power, they brought the barrier down on the far side of Atta. They would lock him into a dome of protection.

Atta pulled himself to stand, shoving Readers out of his way as he made back towards the cave entrance.

The shimmering barrier continued to close in on

him. He picked up speed to escape its encapsulation, but he was not quick enough. As he reached the other side, the barrier slammed down in front of him.

He turned around, but the shield had formed around him. He was trapped.

Chapter 20

The deep blue of the sea in the bay was reflected in the sky. The boat cut through its surface, leaving the gaping mouth of the cave behind, the green shimmer of the temporary barrier that Femi, Stitch and Jay had created still visible as they passed over the Kaapstown sand banks and into deeper waters.

Jay watched over the railing at the back of the old sea ferryboat as Kaapstown grew smaller. Enzo came along beside her. She pointed up into the hills where there were already swathes of people on the move. 'What's that?' asked Enzo. Her pendant hung around her neck, the fragment of source stone grey and lifeless.

'People are getting out,' said Jay, a deep sadness in her tone. The Given had escaped with their lives, but the people of Kaapstown still had a journey of their own. Some would stay. Some might even be converted to the way of the Readers, but most would flee. Mostly, the Readers would leave them be, allow them to migrate, if they were lucky. The surrounding lands would gear up to take them in, help distribute people throughout their own countries. There would be much fear in those countries about the future. Whilst the Readers have no power remote from their source, they will not make good neighbours. Jay felt overcome by their failure to protect Island 7.

'It's not your fault,' Enzo said. 'You did everything you could.' She closed her hand around her pendant and looked up at Jay. Then she opened her hand a crack and a tiny glimmer of green emanated from the stone, a reflection for light from the sun.

Jay smiled and slung an arm around Enzo. She nestled in and they looked out over Kaapstown. 'Cassie told me she buried my dad,' Enzo said. 'But I'll never see his grave.'

'We will come back one day,' Jay said, a tear in her eye for Enzo. 'When this war is over, we will return here.'

Thabisa appeared and smiled warmly at Jay. 'Hey,' she said to Enzo, 'Suki was looking for you. She's down below.'

Enzo ran off and Thabisa leaned up against the railing next to Jay. 'Are you OK?' Jay said, picturing

Thabisa's rage as she beat the Reader who'd killed her husband.

'I might have killed him if Sanata hadn't been there.'

'You've lost a lot.'

Thabisa sighed. 'What's become of us? This is how it ends, with fighting, death...'

Jay looked out at Kaapstown. From a distance, it was peaceful. The sun was setting over on the east side and a warm glow spread over the mountaintops. The green hue would soon darken as the Readers settled deeper into this land. Flora would soon whither and die, retreat below the surface. In time, this would be a dust-land.

'Is this the first time the Dark has prevailed?' asked Thabisa. 'Tiago said we would never be the first to fall to the Readers, and now this.'

'We think this is the first. Some of the other Islands are dark, but not permanently. There is still hope,' said Jay.

'Not here. Kaapstown is lost forever. This will always be the realm of the darkness.' She motioned to walk away but Jay called her back. 'Sorry,' said Thabisa, 'I need to get back to my patients.' Thabisa still had no Given power to heal, but she would do her best to patch people up.

Cassie, Stitch and Femi made their way over to Jay.

'When is someone going to tell us how we're getting home?' said Stitch.

Jay smiled at his tetchiness, her smile quickly dissolving as she knew she'd have to break the news to her friends that they were not going home, not yet.

'Femi said something about Island Five?' said Cassie. She and Femi had been talking a lot since they boarded. Cassie had finally accepted him as one of them, and one of the Given. Jay too had softened towards Femi. He had shown his allegiance to the cause, and he had lost so much to Atta and the Dark. They had killed his mother, Annika, and before that, his father; and they had destroyed his homeland.

Jay looked at Femi and gave him a smile. Back to Cassie, she said, 'We can't go home, not from here. England is halfway around the world.' With Thabisa, Jay had agreed that they should head to another of the eight Islands, where they could replenish their power, and connect with the local Given population. They would need a strong Given source to transport themselves back home, and they had work to do to help protect the neighbouring Islands from further Reader incursion.

'So where to then?' said Stitch. Femi leaned up against the side of the boat. He had already been briefed by Thabisa. Island 6 was the obvious choice, as

Thabisa had informed them it was the closest – only three days by sea. But Island 5 was in trouble.

'Island 5,' said Jay. 'Thabisa has contacts there, and before we lost all Given power on Seven, her fears were confirmed that things had deteriorated on Five. We think the Readers on Five are closing in on the location of the Origin.'

'What about their 8C and their C?' asked Cassie.

'Still alive,' said Jay. 'For now.'

'That's something,' said Stitch.

'Hey,' said Femi. 'I know we didn't get what we hoped for here, but we got something else. We got each other. I haven't said it yet but, thank you. You put your-selves on the line.'

Jay put a hand on Femi's arm. 'We're in this together. And you have taught us a lot. Thank you for your patience.' The dark power within Jay had settled once more now that they were a distance from Kaapstown and the source of Reader energy, but she knew it was there, and she knew much more about the nature of it, and the role it could play in helping the Given to survive in all of their lands. Next time, she will use the integration of the Given and Dark power to its best effect. 'Next time,' said Jay, 'I hope I don't take so long to hear you.' She smiled.

'Hear him,' said Stitch, laughing. 'What about me?

I've been trying to talk to you about this potential for weeks.'

'Yeah right, Stitch, whatever you say,' Jay said, laughing.

'What exactly *was* that back there in the caves?' asked Cassie.

'The shield?' said Femi.

'I was thinking more about the darkness that Jay screamed at that Reader who was about to blow my head off.'

'That was pure, unadulterated anger and determination,' said Jay.

Femi nodded. 'Dark power is different from Given energy. It seems to respond more to emotions, especially anger. The Given power is a holistic force, with multiple strands coming together to join and reinforce one another to create something amazing. The darkness is more singular, focused, and can be very potent.'

'You're telling me,' said Cassie. 'That Reader was pulverised.'

'I'm looking forward to working with you on it, Jay,' said Femi.

Stitch bristled a little and Jay sensed his jealousy. She knew it was wrong, but it made her happy.

Jay turned to face the west and nodded towards the horizon. 'For now, we have a few days to think about what we do when we get there.'

'Island 5,' said Femi, joining Jay to look out west.

Stitch squeezed up in between Jay and Femi, with Cassie on her other side. She smiled at her two friends and looked out to the horizon, considering the energy they would need to muster if they were to face Atta when they got to Five.

The End
(Interland #4)

Thank you!

I hope you enjoyed *The Origin*, book #4 in the Interland series. If you can spare a minute to leave a short review or just a rating on your preferred store, then I'd be very grateful - Thanks!

Leave a review or rating here for The Origin.

If you've not joined my Reader Club, where you can keep up to date on forthcoming publications, news and freebies to go with the INTERLAND series and my other books - including a free eBook prequel called *The Reader*, an insight to the background of the Readers - then please join by visiting my website - www.garyclarkauthor.co.uk

About the Author

Gary graduated from the University of Surrey in the UK with a degree in Engineering, embarking on a career that has taken him all over the world from the Far East to the Americas. He is a graduate of the Faber Academy and Curtis Brown creative writing programmes. Now a father of three, he has settled with his family close to where he grew up on the edge of the South Downs in Sussex, where he indulges his love of books, and passion for writing.

I'd love to hear from you so feel free to contact me on the email address here - let me know what you thought of the book.

Author email: gary@garyclarkauthor.co.uk
Or visit my website: www.garyclarkauthor.co.uk

Made in the USA
Middletown, DE
21 August 2023